TROUBLE AMONG FRIENDS

"I have a job, remember?" Lisa said. "My boss gave me the day off because it was your first day here, but he's expecting me bright and early tomorrow morning. We're shooting some complicated scenes with the horses, and he'll need me."

"Oh, right. Your job." Stevie had almost forgotten about Lisa's summer job with Skye's TV show.

To Carole it was no surprise that Lisa wanted to squeeze every last drop of excitement out of her taste of show business. "I guess you wouldn't want to miss out on one extra minute of that job, right? I'm surprised you could stand to stay away today."

Lisa felt her jaw clenching tightly as she wondered just exactly what Carole meant by that. And what had that odd expression been in Stevie's eyes as she'd said *your job*? Despite the balmy, peaceful surroundings, Lisa was starting to feel a twinge of annoyance with her two best friends.

PINE HOLLOW™

REINING IN

BY BONNIE BRYANT

BANTAM BOOKS
NEW YORK • TORONTO • LONDON • SYDNEY • AUCKLAND

RL5.0, age 12 and up

REINING IN

A Bantam Book / December 1998

"Pine Hollow" is a trademark of Bonnie Bryant Hiller.

ISBN 0-553-49244-6

Published simultaneously in the United States and Canada

Bantam Books are published by Bantam Books, a division of Bantam
Doubleday Dell Publishing Group, Inc. Its trademark, consisting of the
words "Bantam Books" and the portrayal of a rooster, is Registered in
U.S. Patent and Trademark Office and in other countries. Marca
Registrada. Bantam Books, 1540 Broadway, New York, New York 10036.

PRINTED IN THE UNITED STATES OF AMERICA

OPM   0 9 8 7 6 5 4 3 2 1

My special thanks to Catherine Hapka for her help in the writing of this book.

ONE

"Could you pass the coffee, please, Lisa?"

Yawning, Lisa Atwood reached for the white ceramic coffeepot and handed it across the table to her father, who had just taken his usual seat between his wife, Evelyn, and the high chair where Lisa's half sister, Lily, was cooing over a handful of cornflakes. Mr. Atwood reached to take the pot from Lisa, his fingers accidentally brushing the back of her hand.

"Thanks, honey."

Something in his voice made Lisa look up. Squinting sleepily across the small round table, she saw that his eyes looked misty. "Dad?" she said. "What's the matter?"

Mr. Atwood laughed softly and shook his head. He glanced down and busily tightened the belt on his blue terry-cloth bathrobe, though Lisa suspected he was just using that as an excuse to pull himself together. Like Lisa, Mr. Atwood didn't want to let his emotions get the best of

1

him when other people were watching—even his own family.

"Sorry," he said after a moment. "It's just that, well, I was thinking about how nice it is to see you sitting there. In case I haven't said it often enough, it's been really great having you here with us these last couple of months. Almost like old times. Old good times."

"Thanks, Dad." The truth was, he had said it plenty of times. But it was always nice to hear.

"That goes double for me, Lisa." Evelyn reached for the coffeepot, which her husband had set down at her elbow. "We've both gotten used to having you around this place. Lily has, too," she added, shooting a fond glance at the baby. "It won't be the same when you go back to Virginia next week."

"Week after next," Mr. Atwood corrected. He tossed Lisa a wink, all signs of mistiness gone. "Believe me, I'm counting the days."

Evelyn rolled her eyes. "That's what I get for marrying a pointy-headed number cruncher."

Mr. Atwood rubbed his decidedly nonpointy head and pretended to look angry. "Watch it," he growled.

Lisa smiled and glanced at her stepmother. Evelyn's short blond hair was pushed casually off her forehead and her green eyes sparkled as she laughed. The contrast to Lisa's own mother—

with her pallid, unhealthy complexion, the gloomy expression in her eyes, the constant sighs and bitter little remarks—was so strong that it caused an almost physical ache in Lisa's heart. Even though her parents' divorce had been finalized some time ago, Lisa's mother still hadn't managed to pull her life back on course. The quiet, somber mood of Lisa's home in Virginia contrasted sharply with the bright, sunny, relaxed feeling she got sitting in her father's white cottage near the beach in Southern California. When Evelyn noticed Lisa's gaze and met it with a warm, open smile, the contrast increased. The first Mrs. Atwood had never been particularly open or emotionally warm, even with her daughter. These days it seemed she hardly had time for anything except her group therapy—which Lisa secretly called gripe therapy—and long, depressing talks on the phone with Lisa's aunt.

Fortunately Lisa had plenty of other people to lean on for emotional support. There was her father, for one. At the time of the divorce, Lisa had been very angry at him—for leaving them, for moving all the way across the country, for throwing her life into such turmoil. But Mr. Atwood had tried hard to let her know that he still loved her. And finally she had let herself believe him.

Even before that, though, she hadn't had to go

it alone. As always, her two best friends had been there for her. Lisa had met Stevie Lake and Carole Hanson on her first day at Pine Hollow Stables several years earlier, and the three girls had been inseparable ever since. They shared a common bond: horses. When they were younger, Lisa, Stevie, and Carole had spent hours in the saddle.

Now that they were in high school they still loved to hang out at Pine Hollow, though somehow they didn't seem to have as much time for it as they once had—at least Lisa and Stevie didn't. Carole had always been the most serious of the three about all things equine and equestrian, and, true to form, she still managed to spend most of her time at the stable. Lisa smiled as she imagined her friend bustling around Pine Hollow, busy as ever in her summer job as morning stable manager. The job was perfect for Carole, not only because it allowed her to earn some money before her junior year, but also for the jump start it gave her career, which she already knew would have something to do with horses.

Stevie loved horses as much as ever, too, especially her own horse, Belle. But looking back, Lisa now recognized that her impetuous, outgoing friend had always managed to juggle multiple interests while seeming to focus most of her attention on riding. When the girls had first met,

4

Stevie's interests had included playing pranks and practical jokes, fighting with her three brothers, and spending time with her boyfriend, Phil Marsten. These days Phil was still very much in the picture, but Stevie had mostly given up her joking ways, somewhere along the road even reaching a truce with her brothers.

Lisa, for one, was glad about that. Six months earlier, she had suddenly, inexplicably, and undeniably fallen head over heels in love with Stevie's twin brother, Alex. Lisa knew that her friends still didn't understand quite how it had happened, and she wasn't sure she understood it, either. All she knew was that during the dark period following her parents' divorce, one of the few things that had broken through her pain had been strange, disconcerting moments when she would suddenly notice the way Alex's hair curled the wrong way on one side of his forehead, or that his voice had deepened into something that insinuated itself into her mind like a line of music playing over and over again. And once in a while, through the fog that had seemed to surround her during that time, Lisa had noticed Alex looking back at her with an odd, unreadable expression on his face.

Falling in love with Alex had been just the thing Lisa had needed to banish the fog, regain her balance, and return to life. She wished her mother could find a similar lifeline of her own. But she was too sensible to hold out much hope, at least for the foreseeable future.

Mr. Atwood and Evelyn had ended their playful sparring with a quick kiss, and once again peace reigned in the sunny kitchen. Evelyn turned to Lisa with a smile. "Anyway, Lisa, you know what we mean. We'll miss you." She stood and stepped over to Lily's high chair. As soon as she unlatched the spring on the white plastic tray, the baby cooed and held out her arms. Evelyn picked her up and returned to her seat, settling Lily comfortably on her lap. "This visit has been too short."

"The summer has really flown by, hasn't it?" Lisa mused, gazing at Lily. The baby had grown and changed so much even in the short time Lisa had been there. Soon the changes would go on without her there to observe them. "I can't believe it's almost over. I'm not sure I'm ready to leave yet."

"Really?" Mr. Atwood's eyes lit up. "You know, Lisa, if you ever decide—"

"Wait." Lisa held up one hand to silence her father. "Don't start calling in the moving vans yet. It was just an innocent comment. I didn't mean anything by it."

So why did you say it? a little voice in her head

asked. *Since when do you say things you don't mean?*

Lisa didn't know the answer to those questions, so she decided to shove the pesky little voice out of her mind. She could think about it later—like when she was fully awake, for instance. She reached for her coffee cup and took a big swallow.

Mr. Atwood was grinning sheepishly. "Sorry. But you can't blame me for hoping, right? And if you change your mind and decide to leave those cold winters and gray skies for good, you know there are people here in sunny California who miss you like crazy every minute you're gone."

"Right," Lisa replied slowly, thinking of Alex, Stevie, and Carole. "But don't forget, there are lots of people back in Virginia who are missing me right now. And I'm missing them a whole lot, too."

"We know," Evelyn said softly. She rested her chin on Lily's round head. "We never forget you have a mother back East who's counting the seconds until you get home."

Lisa felt a pang of guilt. She hadn't been thinking about her mother at all, just her friends and her boyfriend. Still, as her mother's face floated into her mind, a wave of homesickness swept over her, stronger than any she had felt

7

since arriving in California almost two months earlier.

I guess I miss my mommy, Lisa thought wryly. That wasn't so strange. What was odd was that, try as she might to suppress the thought, Lisa knew she had meant what she'd said: She really wasn't ready to end this California summer. Not yet.

Or maybe that wasn't so strange, since the past two months had been among the most interesting of her life—not to mention being right up there on her personal top ten list of fun times. After all, how many seventeen-year-old girls could say they had worked on the set of a hot new TV show? Lisa knew the job would look very impressive on her college applications next year—almost as impressive as the straight As and other academic honors she had earned over the years.

Then there was all the stuff that wouldn't show up in any college essay, like getting to spend the summer around horses even though she was three thousand miles from Pine Hollow, and working with Skye Ransom, a gorgeous, talented actor just a few years older than Lisa. She had known Skye for years—ever since she and her friends had helped teach him to ride—but it was still a treat to see him. And while Skye was the star of the show, he wasn't the only heartthrob on the set. It seemed that every hot young actor in Hollywood wanted the chance to be a guest star on the show, and Lisa had met them all.

Yes, that sort of thing did a lot to keep her mind off how much she missed her friends back home.

Lisa realized she was thinking so hard that she had missed something her stepmother had just said. "Sorry?" she said. "What was that?"

"I just asked when *Paradise Ranch* debuts," Evelyn said. "You've been slaving away on the set all summer, and the thing hasn't even been on TV yet."

"It debuts in a couple of weeks, and I know exactly what you mean. It's weird that nobody else has even seen the first episode yet. I mean, I feel as though the characters have always been out there. I even know which character gets trampled by stampeding horses in the big Christmas cliffhanger!"

Mr. Atwood threw up his hands in protest. "Don't you dare give it away! We want to enjoy the suspense."

"Don't worry. They swore me to secrecy. If I told you, I'd have to kill you." Lisa glanced at her watch. "Oops. I'd better eat fast if I don't want to be late." She started shoveling her cereal into her mouth as her father and Evelyn chatted about Lily's next doctor's appointment.

Lisa's mind wandered forward. Before long she would be able to watch the premiere of *Paradise Ranch* on TV with her friends back home. She had already e-mailed Alex about it, ordering him to make sure nobody made any other plans for that evening. She could picture it now: She and Alex would snuggle on the Lakes' big, comfortable sofa. Stevie and Phil would be sprawled on the floor in front of the TV set, arms around each other even as they squabbled good-naturedly.

Lisa smiled and sank deeper into the fantasy. Carole would rush in breathless and almost late because she'd waited too long to leave the stable. Phil's friend A.J. would probably come with his girlfriend. Maybe, just maybe, Carole could convince Ben Marlow to join them, if the handsome young stablehand wasn't sunk too deeply in one of his gruff, antisocial moods. Stevie's younger brother, Michael, would probably make fun of the show for days beforehand, but he would be sure to show up just in time to watch it with them. . . .

Lisa sighed as she imagined the scene. She could almost feel Alex's strong arms encircling her, and for a split second she thought she could detect a hint of the aftershave she had bought him.

Then the imagined scent and the picture were gone. Lisa was back in her father's kitchen with a soggy bowl of cornflakes in front of her and the hot California sunshine pouring through the windows. Glancing around, Lisa saw that neither her father nor Evelyn had noticed her day-dreaming. But baby Lily was staring at her from her mother's lap, her small, moist mouth hanging open slightly and her blue eyes wide and curious.

Lisa pushed her cornflakes away. She wasn't hungry anymore.

"Evelyn? Could I hold Lily for a minute before I leave?"

"Definitely." Evelyn stood and held out the baby. "She gets heavier every day. I'm always thrilled when someone else wants to take a turn."

Lisa smiled at her, then hugged Lily tight. "You're the cutest baby in the whole world, you know," she murmured, just loudly enough for Lily alone to hear. "You're not going to forget me when I leave, are you? I promise I'll come visit you as often as I can, and then next summer . . ."

Lisa's voice caught in her throat. Next summer seemed a lifetime away. How could she miss her baby sister so much when she hadn't even left yet?

And no matter how great this summer had been, she couldn't help wondering how she could be so sad that it was ending. After all, Virginia was her home, despite the fact that she fit in a lot better in California than she ever would have expected. Yes, some important parts of her life—her father, her sister, Evelyn, Skye, and other friends—were here. Sometimes those things loomed so large in her mind and heart that it was overwhelming to think of leaving them behind.

But at other times, Lisa yearned to see Alex's face light up the way it always did when he saw her coming toward him. She longed to sink into one of their deep, special, timeless kisses, to feel his hands on the small of her back as they danced to their favorite dreamy, romantic song.

And her friends. She had almost forgotten the precise sound of Carole's distinctive laugh, which always made her sound delighted and somehow surprised at the same time. And it had been too long since Lisa had felt herself being pulled—half unwilling, half expectant—into one of Stevie's big ideas for big fun.

Then there was Pine Hollow. Lisa was sure she had spent as much time on horseback this summer as either of her friends. But she still missed the horse she rode back home, a beautiful Thoroughbred mare named Prancer. She missed the familiar sights and sounds of the stable where she had learned to ride. She even missed hearing Max Regnery, the owner of Pine Hollow, shout corrections at his students.

But thinking about horses made her think about her job, which she loved, and the horses she cared for there, and her interesting new friends. . . .

It was all too much to think about so early in the day. Lisa stood and pushed back her chair, balancing Lily on one hip. "Here you go, baby," she said as cheerfully as she could manage. "Time to go back to Mommy. Your big sister has to go."

As she climbed out of the small red car her father had gotten her for the summer, Lisa heard someone shout her name. She looked up and saw her favorite cameraman waving enthusiastically from the back of his pickup truck, where he was lounging with a tall take-out cup of coffee and the morning paper. Lisa grinned and waved back.

Then she glanced around, still a little bit amazed that this was actually where she worked. It still seemed like a dream sometimes, especially on mornings like this one when the early sun filtered through scattered clouds and left a golden, dappled pattern on everything. One side of the small, dusty parking lot was lined with paddocks. The other opened onto a shaded picnic area, behind which lay the large metal trailers that served as the actors' private changing rooms, rest areas, and offices. Straight ahead, the landscape featured gently rolling fields dotted with an occasional building or piece of television equipment, with rugged foothills rising sharply behind.

With a quick wave to a couple of actors who had just arrived and were heading in the opposite direction, Lisa turned right, heading for the stable area. She had accompanied Skye to studios and sets for a few other TV series during the summer, so she knew that the *Paradise Ranch* set was somewhat unusual. Instead of being housed in a huge, warehouselike building on a studio lot, it was more like a perpetual location shoot. The actors spent some time shooting interior scenes on a soundstage a few miles down the road, but since much of the show took place outdoors, their true home was this dozen or so acres in the foothills of the mountains that bordered Los Angeles, which stood in for the fictional thousand-acre Western guest ranch on which the show centered. The set designers had erected a full-scale post-and-beam farmhouse, several smaller guest cabins, a barn and other outbuildings, as well as marking out areas that represented more farflung parts of the imaginary ranch. Lisa hardly even noticed anymore that the main house was only a few yards from the campsite, though they were supposed to be miles apart, or that the ranch's huge cedar barn had only half a roof and no eastern wall, leaving plenty of space for cameras.

Yes, the set was an interesting place, and Lisa learned fascinating new facts about TV production almost every time she wandered around it. But she had to admit that her favorite spot, as always, was the stable. Unlike the carefully designed buildings that would be seen on the show every week, the stable was a purely functional space. What everyone on the set referred to as the stable was actually a series of long, low, tin-roofed buildings, each containing a row of box stalls overlooking a wide, dusty aisle. A number of paddocks and a spacious, grassy turnout field filled the area between the stable and the two-lane road running past the set.

As Lisa hurried down the path leading to the stable area, she saw a small herd of horses grazing in the big field and several others in the smaller paddocks. That gave her a pretty good idea of the day's schedule, but she glanced at the bulletin board outside the first building to make sure there would be no surprises. Then she set about the familiar tasks involved in keeping several dozen horses fed, watered, groomed, and happy.

Lisa was busy applying hoof oil to the left fore of a pretty chestnut mare named Fancy when Skye Ransom stuck his head over the half door of the stall. "Oh, there you are, Lisa."

Lisa glanced up. As a loyal friend, she thought Skye looked as handsome as ever, though she guessed some of his fans would do a double take if they saw him right then. There were smudges of greenish goo dabbed on several small blemishes on his chin, and a large orange barrette was clamped firmly over the cowlick that constantly frustrated the stylists in charge of taming the young actor's thick blond hair.

As usual, Skye seemed oblivious of how he looked. Unlike some of the other actors working on the show, he never hesitated to wander the set in disarray as long as there were no cameras around to record it. Skye wasn't vain, but he cared about his career. "I wanted to give you some warning," he told Lisa. "The director just told me my first scene today will be the campfire scene. It won't be for a few hours, obviously, because of the light, but . . ."

"But between now and then we have to make sure Topsy looks like he's spent the day on the trail," Lisa finished for him. "Got it."

16

Skye smiled and leaned on the half door. "What did we ever do around here without you? When I recommended you for this job it was because I knew you were good with horses. Who knew you'd turn out to be a natural in this whole TV thing, too?" He winked slyly. "And I'm not the only one who thinks so. I overheard Rick telling the director you're the best assistant he's ever had."

Lisa wasn't sure how to respond to that. She could feel herself blushing. She liked her boss, Rick Santos, and she was pretty sure he appreciated her work. But Rick was a man of few words, so he hadn't actually told her so. "Thanks," she told Skye. "It's easy to do a good job when the work is so much fun. And don't worry about Topsy. By the time he goes in front of the cameras, he'll look as though he spent the day loping along a dusty trail instead of lounging in his stall."

"Thanks, Lisa. I'd better go—I barely glanced at today's lines last night after we all left the pizza place, so I have to get cracking. I'll see you later, okay?" Skye reached over the door and gave Lisa's shoulder a brief squeeze before hurrying off in the direction of his trailer. Even after he had gone, Lisa could still feel the pressure of his hand. She shrugged it off. She and Skye were just friends, no matter what Alex thought. Friends—exactly as they had always been.

She frowned as she thought about the e-mail she had received from Alex the night before. *Thinking of you all the time*, it had read. *Hope you're thinking of me, too, especially when you're looking at the Sky.*

Lisa had tried to tell herself that the capitalization had been an innocent typo. After all, she and Alex had agreed before she left that each of them would look up at the sky each evening at the same time as a way of feeling connected to each other—the same moon, the same stars linking them together across the miles.

But Lisa knew that Alex was jealous of her relationship with Skye. In some ways, she supposed she couldn't blame him. Skye was gorgeous, he was famous, he was wealthy. Still, Alex was the only one she loved. Why couldn't he trust her on that? Some of his comments and questions about Skye could be . . . well, more than a little immature.

"Lisa?" a tentative voice interrupted her thoughts. "Is Fancy ready? I want to practice that rope trick I have to do today before everyone gets here to watch me mess it up."

Lisa started, realizing how ridiculous she must look staring blankly into space, hoof brush in hand, as Fancy nibbled at her shoulder. Luckily the young woman outside the stall hadn't noticed. Summer Kirke didn't notice much that other people did when she was concentrating on her own worries, as she obviously was at the moment.

When she'd first met her, Lisa hadn't thought she would like Summer very much. A large part of the reason had been simple envy. Lisa was sure she had never seen anyone as flawlessly gorgeous as Summer. The young actress played Skye's older sister on the show, and there was some resemblance in the two actors' sunny blond hair and blue eyes. But where Skye's handsome, expressive face had matured in the years that Lisa had known him from that of a boyish teen idol into something stronger, more chiseled and self-assured, Summer's face still retained the rounded edges and smooth, soft innocence of childhood.

If there was one lesson Lisa had learned quickly about the world of make-believe that was the entertainment industry, it was that things weren't always what they seemed. Skye might be a lot like Devon Drake, the charming, easygoing, lovable young heartbreaker he played on *Paradise Ranch,* but Summer bore almost no resemblance to Devon's confident, conniving sister Caitlin Drake. Somehow on camera, though, it all seemed to work.

"Almost, Summer," Lisa said to the young actress. "I can have Fancy ready in about twenty minutes. Is that soon enough?"

Summer brushed a stray strand of golden blond hair off her cheek and nodded gratefully. "Thanks, Lisa. That will be perfect." She smiled, but as she turned to look at the horse, Lisa spotted her lower lip quivering slightly.

Lisa recognized the sign. It meant that Summer was worried or upset about something. She also knew that almost anything could set Summer off. She would burst into tears if her hair didn't look just right, and she practically had hysterics if the director made the mistake of correcting her too sharply. On more than one occasion, even Lisa had been forced to soothe the excitable, hypersensitive actress and assure her once again that she shouldn't take it personally when Fancy misbehaved or one of the other horses put its ears back while looking in her general direction. She was pretty sure that Summer understood intellectually that the horses weren't being purposely mean. But emotionally she had a harder time believing it.

Still, this time Summer's expression worried Lisa. Her lovely, almond-shaped eyes, perfectly framed by long lashes, held an odd expression. . . .

Haunted, Lisa thought. She couldn't help being concerned. In many ways Summer seemed more vulnerable than baby Lily.

"Summer, is everything all—"

"Yo! Lisa!" a voice bellowed.

Lisa bit back an annoyed sigh as she turned to face the newcomer. "Hello, Jeremiah."

Even with everything she knew about him, Lisa had to admit that Jeremiah Jamison was incredibly good-looking. He had the kind of face that made girls all over the world swoon. Deep brown eyes, straight white teeth, thick black hair, and something more, too—a vulnerable, idealistic, deeply soulful expression that cried out for caring and compassion.

Lisa knew better. The only thing Jeremiah cared about was himself. The only compassion he felt was for anyone or anything that could forward his career.

"Do you mind?" Jeremiah gave Summer a dismissive glance. The young woman lowered her eyes and scurried away.

Lisa frowned. She wanted to tell Jeremiah off for his rudeness. She and Summer had been in the middle of a conversation, and he had interrupted, as usual. But she held back, knowing it wouldn't do any good. Quite the contrary, in fact. Jeremiah's quick and nasty temper was infamous around the set, and Lisa had learned the hard way that it was a lot easier just to keep him happy. Easier on her, easier on the horses, easier on the director, easier on everyone.

It's ironic, Lisa thought, listening with half her attention as Jeremiah reeled off a long list of orders concerning his horse, a well-behaved gelding named Jeeves. *Practically any teenage girl in the country—including Stevie or Carole—would trade her left eyeball for the chance to breathe the same air as Jeremiah Jamison. And here I am wishing he'd just go away and leave me alone!* She almost laughed at the thought. But again, she controlled herself. If there was one thing Jeremiah hated more than being contradicted, it was being laughed at.

"Okay, Jeremiah," she said instead as the list of demands ended. "You know you can count on me. I'll have Jeeves ready in plenty of time. Don't worry."

"Good." Jeremiah nodded curtly, then turned and strode away.

Lisa finally let out her sigh of annoyance as she watched him retreat down the stable row. After two months of working with him, she had a hard time believing that most of the world still believed, as she once had, that Jeremiah Jamison was a kind, romantic, sensitive soul. Once *Paradise Ranch* came on the air, that reputation would be even stronger, since he played one of the show's most sympathetic characters, Devon

22

Drake's best friend and resident do-gooder Rand Hayden.

"I hope his publicist is getting paid a lot," she muttered to Fancy, who had stuck her head out into the aisle to see what was going on. Lisa patted the pretty mare on her smooth cheek. "He deserves it."

"Talking to the stock again, Lisa?" a gruff voice said nearby.

Lisa gasped, startled, and whirled to face her boss, Rick Santos. "Fancy was just telling me all about her life as a TV star," she joked weakly.

"Right," Rick drawled. He leaned against a nearby post and hooked his thumbs in the pockets of his well-worn jeans. Then he shrugged casually. "I thought maybe she was telling you how much she'll miss you when you abandon us next week."

"Week after next," Lisa corrected automatically. Then she paused, realizing that Rick had just given her what passed, with him, as a high compliment. Not only had he acknowledged that she was leaving soon, but he had implied that it would be a bad thing. "I'll miss her, too. And everybody else around here."

Rick's dark eyes were shaded by the brim of his ever-present battered Western hat, but the corner of his mouth turned up in a nearly imperceptible smile. "Back atcha, kid." He cleared his throat. "Listen, I wanted to say something. I gave you a shot at this job because Ransom asked me to and because I really needed someone. But you've proved you deserved it."

"Thanks."

"You're young, but you know what you're doing. With horses and people." Rick gave a quick nod, then stood up straight. "I just want you to know I appreciate it. And that Fancy there isn't the only one who'll miss you. You may just be the best stable hand I've ever hired."

Lisa smiled and thanked him again. She ran one hand through her hair as Rick hurried off in the direction of the tack shed. Her boss's words had made her feel great, and not just because he was stingy with compliments. Lisa liked being the best. She had always been that way, which explained her nearly perfect grades and other accomplishments.

But when it came to horses, things were a bit different. At the stable in Virginia, Lisa thought, she didn't get to feel like the best very often. She was always second or third in line behind Carole and Stevie because that was the way it had always been, because they had been riding longer than she had. Nobody except Lisa herself seemed to have noticed that she really wasn't playing catch-up anymore.

Lisa bit her lip, feeling slightly disloyal. Carole

and Stevie were her best friends, and they knew she was a good rider. What did it matter who was better at one thing or another? What kind of a person was she for envying their riding abilities?

Fancy nudged her shoulder, and Lisa stroked the mare's velvety nose. "This seems to be my day for conflicting, messed-up thoughts," she whispered.

Still, after pondering her weird feelings all morning, Lisa had reached a conclusion of sorts. Yes, she missed her mother, her friends, and Alex terribly. But she had to admit that what she had told her father that morning was true. She wasn't quite ready for her wonderful, new, exciting California adventure to end. She didn't know what that meant, but it was true.

"What do you think, Fancy?" Lisa murmured, burying her face in the mare's neck and breathing in the familiar, soothing smell of horse. "Does that make me a horrible person?"

TWO

Carole Hanson glanced at Ben Marlow, Pine Hollow's youngest full-time stable hand. "She looks good. Want to try her at a trot?" She shaded her eyes against the hazy summer sunshine.

Ben nodded. He tossed his head to get his dark, wavy hair out of his eyes, then broke into an easy jog, clucking to the mare at the other end of the lead line he was holding. The mare, a young dapple gray named Firefly, responded with a snort, swinging easily from a walk into a spirited trot.

Carole leaned on the fence of Pine Hollow's outdoor ring, watching the horse critically, paying special attention to her feet. The blacksmith had visited earlier that morning to shoe this latest addition to the stable, and Carole wanted to be sure there were no problems with Firefly's new footwear.

"That's right, girl," she murmured, her eyes

trained on the horse's feet. "All four, square on the ground. That's the way."

Once she had assured herself that the new shoes were fine, Carole allowed herself simply to watch the mare enjoying her exercise. Firefly tossed her head and snorted as she trotted, showing signs of wanting to go faster. But she maintained her pace obediently, her finely shaped head remaining steady above Ben's broad right shoulder.

After a few minutes, Ben stopped the mare and gave her a pat on the withers. "I think she liked that." Carole noticed that he didn't sound the least bit winded from his own exercise in the hot sun.

"Definitely." Carole approached, smiling. "She's quite a horse, isn't she? I'm glad Max bought her. He wasn't going to because she was so expensive—you know, because her sire is that show-jumping champion. But if you ask me, she was worth every penny. She's positively gorgeous!"

"Sure." Ben flicked his fingers at a fly on Firefly's neck. "She's well bred and she's flashy, but she's still raw. We'll have to do some serious training if we really want Max to get his money's worth out of her."

Carole felt herself blushing, realizing that to Ben, her words had probably made her sound like an overexcited schoolgirl. "Right," she said briskly. "That's what I was going to say. I even have some ideas about how to get started. I haven't run them by Max yet, but I know he wants us to get right to work with her and . . ."

I'm babbling and I can't shut up, Carole thought desperately. She tended to do that when she was around Ben. Especially when he stared at her blankly the way he was doing just then . . .

If asked, Carole would have said that she and Ben were friends, bound together by their common, overwhelming love of horses. But sometimes she had to admit that this intense, serious guy was as much a mystery to her now as he had been on his first day at Pine Hollow. Most of the time, when they were working together around the stable, she felt perfectly comfortable with him. But there were other times when he would do or say something—or just give her a certain look with those brooding dark eyes—and leave her completely flustered and confused.

She was glad when she spotted a familiar figure walking slowly up Pine Hollow's long driveway. "Look, there's Stevie," she said, interrupting her own string of words.

Ben turned to look. "She doesn't look too good."

Carole winced. She had to admit that Ben was right. Even from a distance, she could see the glum expression on her friend's face. No, Stevie didn't look good, and she hadn't for some time now.

"It's the accident," she said, though she knew Ben understood that as well as anyone. "She's still dealing with it, even after two months. It's not an easy thing to get over, you know."

Carole realized she sounded a bit defensive, but Ben didn't seem to notice. He just nodded. "These things take time."

It had been a trying period since the car accident that had changed all their lives. Stevie had been driving, and even though there was nothing she could have done to prevent it, that didn't stop her from feeling guilty about it. A horse had died because of the accident, and a girl—a fellow rider their age named Callie Forester—had suffered partial paralysis, which she was still working to overcome. That was a lot for anyone to handle, Carole knew, and she was doing her best to be as strong and supportive as she knew how. But she was secretly starting to wonder if that would be enough. If Stevie wasn't over it by now, would she ever be?

Carole hated seeing her normally upbeat friend look so depressed all the time. She just didn't know how to help her snap out of it. Things had only gotten worse since Phil Marsten, Stevie's longtime boyfriend, had left on a two-week family vacation. With Phil gone, Lisa still far away in California, and Carole busy with her job at Pine Hollow, Stevie had been spending a lot of time alone.

"Besides," Ben said after a moment of silence, "it can't be easy for her to put up with that guy's dirty looks all the time."

Carole didn't have to ask who Ben meant by "that guy." She knew that Ben and Callie's brother, Scott, got along about as well as oil and water. And Scott and Stevie were still uncomfortable around each other. She nodded.

"It's not easy for her to watch Callie struggling to get better and learn to walk again, either," she said quietly. "Or to walk past Fez's empty stall."

She stopped there, since Stevie was almost within hearing range. But her mind didn't stop. It was searching, as it often did those days, for a way to make things better. It was true that Scott Forester, friendly and talkative with everybody else, still fell silent whenever Stevie entered a room. But Callie didn't hold any grudge against Stevie, and neither did Callie's parents. The police had cleared Stevie of any wrongdoing in the accident. Mr. and Mrs. Lake had even bought a new car to replace the one that had been totaled. What else could any of them do? Carole wished Lisa were around to discuss it with her. She was so smart and logical that she would be able to find a solution, if anyone could.

Stevie had reached the ring. "Hi," she said dully. "What are you guys doing?"

Carole gave her a quick rundown of the exercise. "We're almost finished here, though," she said, an idea popping into her mind. "And I'm in the mood for a nice long trail ride as soon as my shift is over. What do you say?" Actually, she had been planning to longe her horse, Starlight, in the ring after she finished working. But that could wait for another day. Stevie needed a lot more help with her mood than Starlight did with his lateral flexing.

Ben looked up. He was still walking Firefly slowly around the ring. Carole hadn't thought he was paying attention to her brief conversation with Stevie, but now it seemed he had heard every word. "It's almost noon," he said, looking Carole in the eye. "Why don't you knock off early and head out now? I'll cover for you."

Carole was surprised. Glancing at her watch, she saw that it was only eleven-thirty. Still, she knew Ben well enough to know that he wouldn't have made the offer if he didn't mean it. "Thanks, Ben."

Stevie looked surprised, too. "Yeah, thanks, Ben." She glanced at Carole, and for a moment a hint of the old Stevie smile flickered across her

31

face. "A trail ride would be nice." Then she sighed. "It's just too bad Lisa isn't here to go with us."

"I know," Carole agreed. The two girls waved good-bye to Ben and wandered toward the stable entrance. "None of our trail rides have seemed complete without her, have they?"

"Nothing seems complete without her. And talking on the phone once in a while doesn't help much. It just reminds us how far away she is."

"I wonder if she misses us as much as we miss her."

"I doubt it. She's probably too busy rubbing shoulders with famous TV stars to think about little old Willow Creek very often."

Carole didn't think that was true. But she had to admit that Lisa's job—in fact, her whole life in Southern California—sounded extremely glamorous. "I wonder what working on that TV show is really like," she mused, trying to imagine it. "Being behind the scenes, working with big stars like Summer Kirke and that hunk, what's his name . . ."

"Jeremiah Jamison," Stevie supplied. "And don't forget Skye."

Carole grinned and glanced over at her friend. "You know, I sort of had forgotten about him. He's such an old friend that he hardly seems like

32

a celebrity, you know? I mean, he's gorgeous and everything, but I hardly even notice that anymore because we know him so well."

"I wonder if Lisa notices," Stevie muttered.

Carole gulped. Suddenly she realized that discussing all the hunks Lisa was working with that summer might not be the safest topic of conversation to have with Lisa's boyfriend's twin sister. "Well, anyway," she said awkwardly, "what I was getting at is that Lisa must be having an interesting time at her job."

Stevie still looked worried. "I just hope she remembers we're all here waiting for her to come home."

This time Carole knew Stevie wasn't thinking of herself or of Carole. She was worried that Lisa would forget she was in love with Alex.

But that would never happen, Carole assured herself. *No matter how many gorgeous Hollywood stars she meets.* "Come on," she said. "Last one to the tack room's a rotten egg."

But Stevie's attention was caught by something new as the two girls rounded the corner. "Ugh," she murmured. "Speaking of rotten eggs, look who's here."

A tall, slender girl with smooth dark hair was coming down the hall toward them, trailed by a good-looking, broad-shouldered young man with wavy blond hair and a rather vacant expression.

"Uh-oh," Carole whispered, recognizing the girl immediately even though she hadn't seen her all summer. "Veronica. What's that snob doing here?"

Veronica diAngelo had once spent a lot of time at Pine Hollow, but she had never even come close to being friends with Carole, Stevie, and Lisa. They had all been in the same riding class, and although Veronica had never been as serious about riding as the others, she had been pretty good at it. Her family was very wealthy, and she had always had top-of-the-line equipment, clothes, and horses. Once she had entered high school, however, Veronica's interest in riding had faded quickly in inverse proportion to her rising interest in the opposite sex. She had sold the last of her accomplished purebred show horses more than two years earlier and dropped out of riding class six months before that. These days she only showed up at the stable occasionally, usually to dazzle a new boyfriend with her still-impressive riding skills.

"Hello, girls," Veronica said breezily. "Long time no see. Do you know Trent?" She gestured at the hunk behind her.

Too bad Veronica couldn't stay away longer,

34

Carole thought automatically. But she returned the greeting politely.

"How are you, Stevie?" Veronica continued smoothly.

"Fine." Stevie's reply was curt. She and Veronica no longer fought like cats and dogs as they once had, but that didn't mean they liked each other. At Fenton Hall, the private school both attended, the two girls generally tried to avoid each other as much as possible. That wasn't difficult—they didn't exactly travel in the same circles.

"Good." Veronica's expertly made-up eyes shifted from Stevie's face to her faded, wrinkled blue jeans and then to her manure-stained T-shirt. In the old days, Carole knew, Veronica wouldn't have been able to resist a snide comment on Stevie's wardrobe. But now Veronica just wrinkled her nose slightly, then fingered the collar of the stylish linen shirt she was wearing. "I see you're still spending all your time hanging around this place, just like when we were kids."

Carole winced. She should have known this encounter couldn't go completely smoothly. There was too much water under the bridge for that. Cold, rancid, polluted water.

Stevie shrugged. "Hey, it beats the mall." Only the slightest narrowing of her eyes revealed her annoyance. "I guess the only drawback is there aren't enough guys here to find a new one to date every week." She paused and smiled sweetly. "But then, I've never been into that like some people are."

Noticing the perplexed look on Trent's square-jawed face, Carole swallowed a nervous giggle. She and Lisa attended Willow Creek's public high school, so they didn't often get to observe Veronica's love life firsthand. But Stevie had kept them well informed, describing how Veronica had a different guy on her arm for every party or dance. Lisa's theory was that this was a result of Veronica's snobby, shallow personality combined with her short attention span.

A brief look of irritation crossed Veronica's pretty face, but she didn't reply. Carole was relieved—in Stevie's current state, the last thing she needed was a revival of her feud with Veronica.

"What are you doing here, Veronica?" Carole put in quickly, trying to head off any further exchange between the other two girls.

"Trent and I are here for a ride, and —Oh, hello. I don't think we've met."

Carole turned to see who had caused Veronica to interrupt herself and saw Ben coming down the aisle, Firefly's equipment slung over one arm. She frowned, not liking the appraising look in Veronica's eyes as she looked at Ben. "This is

Ben Marlow," she told Veronica curtly. "He works for Max." She figured that would end any interest Veronica had in Ben, since her tastes ran more to guys with platinum cards and trust funds than any mere mortal who had to work for a living.

"Hello there, Ben Marlow," Veronica cooed. "I'm Veronica diAngelo. I used to ride here all the time." She gave Ben a long, lingering look that made Carole blush—though to all appearances, Ben didn't even notice it. "Looks like maybe I stopped too soon."

"Anyway, Veronica," Carole put in quickly, her face burning, "if you were looking for Max, I think he's up at the house right now, but Red is probably—"

"Whatever." Veronica didn't let her finish. "I was just looking for someone to tack up a couple of horses for Trent and me. You're working here now, right, Carole?"

Carole frowned. One of Max's firmest rules was that riders had to do their own work, from tacking up to mucking out stalls. Veronica knew that as well as Carole did. Then again, Veronica hadn't put much stock in that particular rule even when she had ridden there regularly.

Stevie wasn't paying much attention to the conversation. She was doing her best to fight down her sudden, burning urge to shout insults at Veronica. The urge was so strong it was almost scary.

What's my problem? Stevie demanded of herself, her fists clenched at her sides as Veronica smoothly ordered Carole and Ben to tack up horses for her and her blockhead boyfriend. *I mean, since when do I care what Veronica diAngelo thinks of the way I dress? It's not like she hasn't said a million worse things to me over the years.*

For some reason, though, this whole conversation was bugging her a lot more than it should. Stevie wanted to leap at Veronica and punch her right in her snooty upturned nose.

I guess Mom and Dad are right when they say I'm a little on edge these days, Stevie thought ruefully. Suddenly her angry feelings evaporated, so fast that she was left feeling limp and empty. This wasn't about Veronica at all. Veronica didn't matter. It was all about the accident. Stevie's whole life these days was about that one horrible moment when she had lost control of that stupid car.

Trying to distract herself from her own thoughts, which seemed to run in a circle—a circle that always brought her back to the same place—Stevie returned her attention to the conversation going on around her.

"Fine." Carole was glaring at Veronica, her face tight and annoyed. "Ben and I will drop everything and throw a saddle and bridle on a couple of horses for you. Even though we have about a million other things to do."

"Good." Veronica linked her arm through Trent's and smiled up at him. "I think Trent would love to ride that big gelding, Congo. And I'm dying to try that pretty gray mare I saw in the paddock when I drove by last week. I don't know her name, but she's a dapple gray with a big white star."

Carole looked more annoyed than ever at that, and Stevie knew why. The dapple gray was Firefly, of course—it figured that Veronica would demand to ride the newest, most expensive horse in the stable. Congo, a large, steady gelding, was actually a good choice for Trent, who didn't look like a very experienced rider. Still, anyone but Veronica would have allowed the stable staff to recommend a horse for him rather than choosing one herself.

"I don't know about that. Both those horses have already been exercised today." Carole's face was taking on a stubborn look that Stevie recognized—one that meant she was getting ready to fight to the death for a horse's safety or well-being.

Looks like I'm not the only one who's overreacting to Veronica today, Stevie thought wryly. She knew it wouldn't hurt Firefly or Congo to spend a leisurely hour on the trail.

Ben obviously agreed with her. "It'll be okay, Carole," he said calmly. "We didn't work Firefly very hard just now."

"But they could just as easily ride Barq and Patch, who haven't been worked today at all," Carole said, still looking mulish.

"Patch?" Veronica's nose wrinkled again. "You mean that poky old thing is actually still alive? He was already about a hundred when I used to ride here. Don't try to pawn off your senior citizens on us. We want to have some fun out there."

Looking downright irate, Carole opened her mouth to respond. But Ben beat her to it. "No problem," he said. "Carole and I will have Firefly and Congo ready in no time." He headed for the tack room without even glancing back to see if Carole was following.

She was. After shooting an angry glare in Veronica's direction and a perplexed glance at Ben, she hurried after the stable hand.

"Thanks so much," Veronica called to them cheerily. "We'll meet you out front."

Stevie shook her head in amazement. Veronica clearly hadn't changed much. She still loved getting her own way. Stevie wondered if that might help to explain the short duration of her romantic relationships. Maybe the guys she went out with got fed up with being ordered around and ducked out after a date or two. *Probably not,* she decided. *If Veronica ever wanted to get serious with a guy, she'd probably just order him to buy her the Hope Diamond as an engagement ring.* Her mouth twisted slightly. *And he'd probably do it.*

"So what have you been up to lately, Stevie?" Veronica asked, her voice just a little too casual. "Having an interesting summer?"

Stevie started. She had almost forgotten that the two of them were alone now. Well, except for Trent, and he didn't really count. She glanced at the tall, handsome guy beside Veronica. His mouth had fallen open just a little, and his eyes looked dull and unfocused as he stood waiting for something to happen.

Stevie turned her attention back to Veronica. The look in her eyes was one that Stevie hadn't seen directed her way in a long time, but she recognized it just the same. It was that certain cool, slightly predatory expression that Veronica got when she was in the mood for trouble. Stevie was instantly on guard.

"Sure," she said lightly, trying to keep the tension she felt out of her voice. The last thing she wanted to do was let Veronica diAngelo, of all people, see how thin-skinned and wounded she was feeling these days. That would be like beg-

41

ging for torture and humiliation. She turned and started walking down the aisle toward the entryway, hoping Veronica would take the hint and leave her alone. "Nothing special."

"Oh, really?" Veronica wandered along beside her. She glanced over at Trent, who was dutifully keeping pace, then back at Stevie. "I heard you got your driver's license."

Stevie gritted her teeth, wishing she had gone to help Carole and Ben with the horses. "Look, it's been nice talking to you and everything. But I have to—"

"Oh!" Trent's dull blue eyes suddenly lit up with interest. "I get it, Ronnie. This is that girl you were talking about, right? The one who caused that accident."

"I didn't cause—" Stevie cut herself short, willing herself to remain calm.

Veronica was giving her a crocodile smile, gazing at her through slightly lowered eyelids. "That's right," she told Trent lightly. "It was all over the news, remember? The police said Stevie wasn't responsible for killing that horse and paralyzing that girl. Who was she again, Stevie? A congressman's daughter? Or was it a senator's?"

Stevie paused just inside the stable door. She could hear the blood pounding in her veins and feel her hands starting to shake. Was it always going to be this way? Weren't people ever going

42

to get tired of talking about the accident? And wasn't she ever going to be able to discuss it without this horrible rush of emotions?

Sometimes Stevie thought it would be easier to run away to someplace new, where nobody had ever heard of her or Callie Forester or any of it. That way she wouldn't have to deal with the constant reminders, the thoughts and memories and nightmares. . . . It was bad enough when well-meaning people asked polite questions about it. But to be taunted—however subtly— by not-so-well-meaning people like Veronica was almost unbearable. Still, she knew what she had to do. She had to be the mature one, the one to take the high road. She couldn't let her feelings show, no matter what.

"Like I was saying," she said at last, through clenched teeth, "I'd better go see if Carole needs any help."

Veronica shrugged. "Whatever. Just remember, if you need anyone to talk to about this, I'm here for you, Stevie."

The offer was so ridiculous—and so clearly hypocritical—that Stevie almost laughed. That helped for a second, making it easier to stick to her vow not to let Veronica see that any of this was bothering her.

But at that moment, she heard voices coming

toward them from the direction of the front doors. Familiar voices.

With a sinking feeling, Stevie turned and saw Callie and Scott Forester entering the stable. Callie was leaning heavily on her brother's arm. He was carrying her crutches in his free hand and moving slowly to let her keep up. Callie's face was twisted with effort as she struggled to move her limp right leg with every step.

Both of them spotted Stevie right away. Callie gave her a quick wave and a smile, but Scott stared at her coldly for a moment before turning deliberately away, his face set in stone.

That was the last straw. It was all too much for one person to take. The torture was never going to end. Things were never going to go back to normal. What was the point of pretending? Stevie's will crumbled, the despair rose up and overwhelmed her, and to her own intense humiliation she suddenly burst into tears. "I've got to go," she sobbed, feeling like the world's biggest loser as she shoved past an astonished Veronica. "I have to go home now."

THREE

"Just wait until Lisa hears Veronica was hanging around again," Carole whispered to her horse, Starlight. Starlight snorted as if in reply and nudged her side with his big, soft nose, clearly looking for treats. Carole smiled and pulled out a piece of apple. As she fed it to him, she felt a little of the tension in her body melt away.

"I knew you'd help calm me down, boy," she murmured, giving the bay gelding a hug.

If there was one constant in Carole's life, it was that she could always count on horses to help get her through any problem, great or small. It was riding that had allowed her to pick up the pieces and go on after her mother had died when she was eleven years old. And now it was a horse that was calming her down after her irritating encounter with the queen of irritating encounters, Veronica diAngelo.

It's all just part of the job, Carole reminded

herself, still stroking Starlight's glossy coat. *Working with horses doesn't guarantee I won't have to work with annoying people sometimes.*

She laughed. That last bit of advice sounded exactly like something logical, coolheaded Lisa might say.

"I bet Lisa doesn't have to deal with jerks like Veronica at her job," Carole told Starlight. "She gets to hang out with movie stars all day long and take care of totally gorgeous horses on top of it."

As she said it, she felt a twinge of envy. But she shook it off. She wasn't that kind of person, was she? Just because one of her best friends was spending her summer vacation hanging out in Hollywood, while Carole was in Virginia, mucking out stalls and saddling horses for lazy, snobby—

"Never mind," she interrupted her own self-pitying thoughts sharply. Starlight's ears swiveled toward her attentively, and she gave him one last pat before letting herself out of his stall. "I guess Stevie isn't the only one around here who needs a nice, long, relaxing trail ride. I'll be back as soon as I find her, boy."

Carole hurried down the aisle toward Belle's stall, shaking her head to clear it. Her envious thoughts had already fled. She was genuinely happy that Lisa had the opportunity to enjoy such an interesting summer. She only wished she could have had it in Willow Creek with her and Stevie. Still, Lisa would be coming home soon—the week after next. Then everything could go back to normal.

Stevie wasn't with Belle, so Carole headed for the tack room, hoping that her friend was already getting ready for the trail ride. She didn't find her in the square, leather-scented room, but she did find Ben. He was seated on a trunk, bent over a grungy bridle strap.

"Hi," she said. "Did Veronica and her little friend get off okay?" She had tacked up Congo as Ben prepared Firefly but hadn't hung around to watch Veronica and Trent mount. She had been too annoyed.

Ben nodded. For a moment he didn't seem inclined to elaborate. But just as Carole was about to ask if he'd seen Stevie, he spoke. "You didn't tell me that girl knew how to ride. I watched for a minute or two because I thought Firefly might be too much for her. But she's really good."

Carole could hardly believe it. Was that actually admiration in Ben's voice?

"Sure," she replied, her own voice dripping with sarcasm. "She ought to be good. She had the best riding instruction money could buy." She took a deep breath. "But I didn't come here

47

to talk about her. I'm looking for Stevie. Have you seen her lately?"

"Actually, Veronica said something about—"

Carole cut him off before he could finish. "Enough about Veronica already, okay?" she said sharply. "She's taken up enough of my time today. If you don't know where Stevie is, I'd better keep looking." Ignoring the surprised look on Ben's face, she stomped off to check Belle's stall once more.

Carole was patting Stevie's lively mare on the nose and wondering where to look next when Denise McCaskill came rushing up to her. "Carole! I'm so glad you haven't left yet!" the young woman exclaimed, looking relieved.

"Hi, Denise." Carole glanced at her watch, realizing that it was well after noon. Her shift was officially over—especially now that she knew Denise had arrived. Denise was finishing the last few credits she needed for her bachelor's degree in equine studies. She spent her mornings in class, hurrying from the school to Pine Hollow for her job as afternoon stable manager. Soon she would be ready to take on a full-time job at the stable. Carole was happy about that, but she knew at least one person who was even happier. Red O'Malley, the head stable hand at Pine Hollow, was Denise's longtime boyfriend. "What's

48

up?" Carole asked, noting the look of consternation on Denise's normally calm face.

"Checkers let himself out of the paddock again."

"Again?" Carole sighed. The mischievous quarter horse was a real escape artist. A horse-proof bolt kept him in his stall, but he still managed to steal out of Pine Hollow's fields and paddocks on a regular basis. "What did he do this time?"

"What *didn't* he do?" Denise replied grimly. "By the time we noticed he was out—by the way, don't ask me how he opened that new gate latch, since the guy who sold it to Max swore it was horseproof—he had had quite a spree. He knocked down most of those new baby trees Deborah planted behind the paddock. He let himself into the grain shed and sampled some alfalfa pellets—after he tore apart the sack, of course. We're also pretty sure he's the one who opened the gate to the side paddock and let that pair of yearlings into the big field. And to top it off, when we finally tracked him down, he was busy rolling in the manure pit."

"Ick." Carole wrinkled her nose. Even with all her experience, some of the things horses did still amazed her. *It's incredible when you think about it,* she thought. *Each one really does have its own unique personality, and sometimes . . .*

Suddenly she noticed the pleading, expectant look Denise was giving her. "Oh. I guess you probably need some help, right?"

"Sorry," Denise said. "I know your shift is over. But this is going to be a big job, and Max wants all hands on deck."

"No problem. I'm right behind you." Carole sighed. First Veronica, and now this. At this rate, starting school in a few weeks was going to feel like a vacation. "So much for that trail ride," she muttered as she followed Denise down the aisle.

Stevie wanted nothing more than to lock herself in her room and cry for a week.

"I shouldn't be this freaked out," she muttered as she cut across a neighbor's yard. She figured if she said it out loud, maybe she would start to believe it. "The stupid accident happened two months ago."

But saying it didn't help any more than thinking it had. Stevie just couldn't seem to put the accident behind her. She had to admit things were at least a little better than they had been at first—there were days now when she managed to forget what had happened for whole hours at a time. But she also still had moments, like this one, when her emotions were so intense she could hardly stand it. At those moments it was as if the accident had happened yesterday, even five minutes before. She wondered if she would ever really get over it. How could she, when everywhere she turned there was another reminder? Every time she saw Scott or Callie, every time she turned the key in the ignition, every time it rained . . .

Stevie rubbed her forehead wearily and blinked back a few stray tears as she turned up her family's driveway, heading for the front door. Why did this have to happen to her? It wasn't fair. She hadn't done anything to deserve this. She was a good driver, a good person . . .

The phone was ringing as she let herself into the front hall. From upstairs, she heard her mother's voice calling faintly for someone to pick up.

"What timing," Stevie murmured, hurrying into the living room to grab the phone off the small table beside the sofa.

As her hand touched the receiver, a sudden irrational feeling swept over her. It was Lisa on the other end of the line, she was positive. Lisa was calling because she knew Stevie needed her. Hearing her friend's voice was just about the only thing Stevie could imagine that might cheer her up right then. Hearing her voice, and hearing that Lisa had booked a nonrefundable ticket back to the East Coast, that she couldn't wait to get back home to Willow Creek where she belonged . . .

"Hello?" she said eagerly into the receiver, waiting for the familiar voice to greet her in return.

But the voice that came wasn't familiar. It was a woman's voice, brisk and businesslike. "Hello there. I'm calling for Ms. Stephanie Lake, please."

"This is Stevie Lake," Stevie replied automatically, feeling a little confused that such a strong premonition had turned out to be false.

"Hello, Steph—er, Stevie." The woman's voice suddenly sounded much warmer. "This is Elsie Summers from WCTV. We met a couple of months ago after you—after Congressman Forester's daughter was injured in that car crash."

"I remember you," Stevie said numbly. She sank down onto the couch, her legs weakening as a feeling of déjà vu overtook her. Elsie Summers was a reporter for the local television station. She had done a whole series of reports on Stevie's accident, asking nosy question after nosy question. She had called Stevie's house several times a day. She had tracked down the driver's ed teacher from Stevie's school to interview him about what kind of student Stevie had been. She had even brought a camera crew to Pine Hollow,

52

though Max had refused to let them onto the property. For a while, Stevie had learned to expect to encounter the pushy reporter every time she turned around. The woman had even started turning up regularly in Stevie's nightmares. Stevie's parents had been on the verge of taking legal action against the TV station when a local farmer had dug up three human skeletons in his cornfield. That had distracted Elsie Summers enough to make her forget about Stevie. Stevie had thought that this particular part of her ordeal, at least, was over. So what did Elsie Summers want from her now?

"I hope I'm not calling at a bad time," the reporter went on smoothly. "But I realized that it's been a couple of months since the accident, and I thought our viewers would want to know how things are going for you and Ms. Forester. I understand she's undergoing physical therapy. That's why I want to do a follow-up piece. It will make a terrific human interest story, don't you think?"

Stevie gritted her teeth. She couldn't believe it. Wouldn't people ever get tired of talking about one lousy car accident? Wasn't there anything of greater importance happening in the world? Wouldn't Stevie ever have any peace?

"No, I don't think it would," she said evenly,

her hand clenching the phone receiver in a death grip. "I definitely don't."

"Oh, but I can assure you, people are very interested," Elsie Summers insisted. "Why, I've received several letters and calls this week alone about your story. People are very concerned."

That was all Stevie could take. She could feel her face turning lobster red, but she didn't care. "Then why don't you tell them to mind their own business?" she shouted. "And while you're at it, why don't you tell yourself that, too?" She slammed the phone down so hard that the plastic casing cracked. Then she buried her face in her hands and started to sob.

"Stevie! What was all that shouting?" Mrs. Lake appeared in the living room doorway a moment later. When she saw that Stevie was crying, she hurried over, sat down beside her, and hugged her, cradling her to her shoulder. "What's the matter, Stevie? Did something happen? Who was that on the phone?"

"It was that reporter from Channel Fourteen," Stevie replied thickly. Her hands were shaking, even wrapped in her mother's firm grip, and she couldn't stop them. "The one that did all those awful stories about me after the accident."

Mrs. Lake's expression grew grim. "You mean Elsie Summers?" She shook her head. "I knew we should have done more about her intrusiveness." Her face softened as she looked at her daughter. "I'm sorry, honey. I'm sorry we couldn't do more to stop all that mess after the accident. I thought it was over."

Stevie and her mother had always been close. As the only two females in their large household, they shared a special bond. In the past, Stevie had been able to tell her mother just about anything. Now, raising her tear-streaked face to Mrs. Lake's sympathetic one, Stevie recognized for the first time that she had been holding back these past two months. She'd shared some of her pain with her parents, but not all of it. Not even close. She supposed it was because she'd felt it shouldn't be such a big deal. After all, Callie was the one who'd been hurt. Stevie had walked away with just a few minor injuries that had long since healed.

But after what had just happened, Stevie realized she needed help. Her body might have healed, but the hurt inside her soul wasn't getting better by itself. Maybe her mother could help, maybe not. The least Stevie could do was tell her the truth.

She let all the emotions of the past two months pour out in a rush. She told her mother about the nightmares that still came a couple of times a week. About the cold looks she got every time she saw Scott Forester. About the overwhelming feelings of guilt and sadness and worry that practically paralyzed her when she watched Callie struggle to walk again. Mrs. Lake sat quietly through it all, listening and stroking Stevie's hair with one hand while holding both her hands tightly with the other.

". . . so I guess there's something really wrong with me," Stevie finished at last, feeling as wrung out as a well-worn rub rag. "I thought time was supposed to heal all wounds or something like that. But a lot of time has passed, and things aren't getting much better, and I feel like I don't have any control over anything, like helping Callie or getting Scott to forgive me."

"You can't control what other people think or feel, sweetie," Mrs. Lake said softly. "Only yourself."

Stevie shrugged. "I guess I can't do that, either." She loosened one of her hands from her mother's grip and swiped at her eyes. "I know the accident wasn't my fault. It could have happened to anyone, and I did what I had to do, and it could have been worse, and all that stuff. I thought I'd made peace with it. And if it were just up to me, I think maybe I could. I mean, Callie forgave me ages ago, and she's really the only one that should matter, right? But it's hard to remember that when I feel like there are so many other people watching and judging. . . ."

She could feel her lower lip trembling. She bit down on it, hard, to make it stop. She didn't want to start bawling again.

Her mother watched her closely, looking concerned. "I had no idea this was still so hard on you. I wish you'd said something sooner." She shook her head. "But never mind. All we can do is start from today and see what we can do."

"I don't think there's anything we *can* do," Stevie muttered with a sniffle.

"Well, we can try." Mrs. Lake paused, thinking. "Maybe it would help if you could get away from all the things that are reminding you of the accident. You know, have a little fun before school starts. How about a family vacation?"

"A family vacation?" Stevie repeated dubiously. "You mean like going to Disney World or King's Dominion or someplace?" Normally she loved amusement parks. But somehow she didn't think screaming her head off on a roller coaster or two was going to change the way she felt. *Of course, hanging around here hasn't been much of a picnic, either,* she reminded herself glumly.

Mrs. Lake shrugged. "I was thinking more along the lines of a week camping in the mountains. But actually, now that I think about it, your father has that big case coming up next week, and he's afraid it's going to drag out all month—"

The sound of the back door slamming interrupted her. A moment later Alex loped into the living room. He stopped short when he saw his mother and sister huddled on the couch. "Hi. What's going on?"

"Nothing," Stevie said quickly, moving a few inches away from her mother. She didn't want any of her brothers to know how hard she was taking this. It wasn't as if they would tease her the way they had when they were all younger. But she didn't want their pity, either.

Mrs. Lake seemed to sense how she felt. "We were just talking about how we haven't taken a family trip in a long time," she told Alex. "I thought it would be nice if we could all do something special before school starts. I don't think your father can get away for long, but what if we all went away over the weekend? Maybe the beach . . ."

"No can do," Alex said immediately. "Half the county is having Labor Day parties, and they all just realized their yards need a ton of work before then. I'm going to be at it nonstop for the next two weeks. I'll be lucky if I can take a break long enough to eat dinner once in a while."

Mrs. Lake sighed. "Well, maybe we can come up with something else. . . ."

The phone rang again. Stevie jumped, badly startled by the sudden noise. "I can't get that!"

she cried, ignoring the confused look on Alex's face. "It's probably that reporter calling back."

"I'll get it." Mrs. Lake's face was stern as she picked up the receiver. "Hello, Lake residence. . . . Oh!" Her expression softened. "Hello, Lisa. It's nice to hear your voice after all this time."

Stevie's heart jumped. "It's Lisa?" she said excitedly, reaching for the phone. Alex, too, had taken a couple of steps forward, his face eager.

Mrs. Lake held up a hand. "Just a second," she told her children. Then she spoke into the phone again. "Lisa? Stevie and Alex are here, and they're both dying to talk to you. But first, I have a question for you. Could you and your father use a visitor for a few days? Because I think I have just the girl for you . . ."

For a second the words didn't sink in. Then Stevie gasped. "Really?" she cried. "You'd really send me to California?" Her gloom lifted a little. Hadn't she just been thinking that Lisa could be the one to help her through her problems?

"Hey!" Alex protested. "What about me? I miss Lisa, too!"

"You'll be working nonstop, remember?" Mrs. Lake winked at Stevie and allowed Alex to wrestle the phone away from her.

For once, Stevie didn't mind letting her brother talk first. She smiled at her mother, feeling happier than she had in a long time. Soon she would be able to talk to Lisa all she wanted—in California. She would be able to see for herself what was so great about the West Coast. And best of all, she would be there to help Lisa pack to come home, thereby bringing this whole confusing, tumultuous summer to a close once and for all.

"I still can't believe I'm going, too," Carole said into the phone.

"I know," Lisa replied from the other end of the line. "Isn't it great? The three of us will have almost a whole week to hang out here. You'll get to meet Evelyn and Lily, see Skye . . ."

"And you. Don't forget, you're the main reason we're coming." Carole sighed happily as she settled back against the sofa cushions in her living room. This had all happened so fast. Just a little more than twenty-four hours earlier, she had been at Pine Hollow, searching for Stevie. Now she was practically on her way to the West Coast and days and days of hanging out in gorgeous California sunshine, enjoying some of the glamour and luxury she had been picturing all summer. It had been Mrs. Lake's idea: She thought that if Stevie had her two best friends with her, she'd be more likely to relax and enjoy the trip. Luckily she had been able to convince

Carole's father, who was almost as crazy about Stevie as if she were his own daughter, to cough up some of the frequent flier miles he'd earned from the cross-country speaking engagements he'd been doing since retiring from the Marines. Luckier still, Denise had been downright eager to start her full-time job at Pine Hollow a couple of weeks early, so Carole was off the hook with Max, too.

"I just hope Alex doesn't hold this against us too much." Lisa sounded worried.

Carole shrugged and twined the phone cord around her finger. In her opinion, Alex would just have to deal with it. "I think he understands that Stevie really needs this right now," she said. "Besides, from what Stevie told me, there's no way he could get away. He's already committed to all those lawn jobs."

Lisa sighed, and Carole guessed that she was missing Alex a lot. "Anyway," Lisa said, "it's probably better this way. It sounds like Stevie really needs a break from everything that reminds her of home."

"Except us," Carole added immediately. "But you're right. She's really had a tough time these past two months."

"Don't worry. If anything can cheer her up, it's the friendly people, blue skies, and gorgeous beaches we've got out here."

Carole raised an eyebrow, a little surprised. What did Lisa mean, *we?* It almost sounded as if Lisa was thinking of California as home. Carole quickly shrugged the idea off. "Sure," she said. "It sounds like you've been having fun. You know, partying with movie stars and everything."

Lisa laughed. "Well, TV stars, anyway. And it's been great. But don't forget, they're just people like you and me."

"Right," Carole said sarcastically. "I'm so sure that Skye Ransom and Jeremiah Jamison have *everything* in common with a bunch of snot-nosed Pony Clubbers who all want to ride Patch at every lesson. And of course, Summer Kirke must be *exactly* like old Mrs. Twitchett, who starts screaming bloody murder if her horse breaks out of a walk."

Lisa laughed again. "Hey, I didn't say things here were *exactly* the same," she protested. "For instance, back in Willow Creek I'm not just a fifteen-minute walk from the beach. I can't wait to show you guys around. You'll love it here. I know you will."

"Great." Carole kept her voice bright, but suddenly she didn't feel quite as excited as she had a few moments before. She bit her lip and picked at the fabric of the sofa. Was it her imagination or did Lisa sound awfully high on this whole California-living thing? Now that Carole thought back over their conversation, Lisa had seemed a lot more interested in talking about all the great things out there than she was in missing the great stuff back home. Could that be true? Or was Carole just being paranoid? Was Lisa thinking of California as home? There was only one way to find out, and that was to ask her about it.

Before Carole could figure out how to broach the subject, she heard a gasp from the other end of the line.

"What?" she asked. "What's wrong?"

Lisa let out another laugh, though it was a bit high-pitched and nervous. "Oh, it's nothing," she said breathlessly. "Just a tremor."

That made Carole sit up straight on the couch. She gripped the phone hard. "A tremor?" she repeated. "You mean, like an earthquake?" She remembered that when Lisa had called them during Callie Forester's party, she'd said something about a tremor then. Now she was experiencing another one. Suddenly Carole thought these tremors were getting a little too frequent. She knew California had earthquakes, but that was something it hadn't even occurred to her to worry about—that the earth could open up and swallow Lisa whole at any moment. *There are no earthquakes in Willow Creek,* she thought.

This time Lisa's laugh sounded more genuine. "It's over already," she announced. "Don't worry. It wasn't the Big One this time, I guess."

Carole forced herself to chuckle in return. "Good," she said. "Well, I guess I'd better go before Dad realizes how long we've been talking and decides to cash in those frequent flier miles to pay the phone bill."

The two girls said good-bye, and Carole hung up. But she sat still for a few minutes, thinking hard. Something about the conversation had left her feeling unsettled. Maybe it was just the earthquake tremor. That had been pretty weird, talking to Lisa at the same time the ground was shaking under her feet. It had to be what was bothering her.

Then again, maybe that was only part of it.

FOUR

"*And this is the beach,*" *Lisa said, pointing to a glistening stretch of pure white sand.* "*See? It's just steps away from home.*" *She waved a hand down the trail at the enormous, sprawling white modern house they had just left.*

"*Neat,*" *Stevie said cheerfully.* "*I'm so glad we came to visit.*"

Carole nodded in agreement. The beach was beautiful. So were the majestic mountains rising directly behind the walking trail where the girls were standing and the towering California redwoods all around them. From somewhere in the distance, Beach Boys music drifted toward them on the breeze.

Carole breathed deep, enjoying the scene. But then she felt something odd under her feet.

"*L-Lisa?*" *she stammered uncertainly.* "*Um, was that a—a tremor?*"

Lisa laughed carelessly and waved her hand in the air. "*Don't worry about it!*" *she exclaimed.*

"Nobody around here even notices a little tremor or two."

Carole gasped as the ground rumbled under her feet once again. This time she heard it as well as felt it—an ominous crunching, grinding sound.

Now Stevie looked worried, too. "Was that another tremor?"

Lisa shrugged, looking slightly irritated. "Would you two stop yammering on about tremors?" she said. "I want to teach you how to surf before we have to leave for the movie premiere tonight. And don't forget, we have reservations afterward at that hot new restaurant on Rodeo Drive where all the most famous movie stars hang out, and—"

"Eek!" Carole squawked as the dirt beneath her feet buckled and swelled. This time there was no mistaking it, and this time it didn't stop. The trail in front of them lifted and swayed as if there were some monstrous creature beneath it that had just awakened and was struggling to burst out.

Stevie's face had gone white. She took a deep breath. "Earthquake!" she screamed at the top of her lungs.

Carole was too scared to scream. She grabbed at the trunk of a nearby redwood for support, but even as she did, it started to topple sideways. Carole threw herself on the ground, hardly daring to look as a gaping fissure suddenly yawned open just a few yards in front of them and huge boulders started to

66

roll down the hillside. She could feel her whole body shaking along with the tortured earth . . .

"Carole! Wake up!"

Carole's eyes flew open. She still felt herself being yanked back and forth. But now she saw the real reason why. Stevie was shaking her briskly by the shoulder, peering impatiently into her face.

"Uh—wha—?" Carole murmured, twisting her shoulder out of Stevie's firm grip and rubbing her eyes. She glanced around the crowded interior of the jumbo jet. She and Stevie were seated in the center row, so she couldn't see out the windows. "Are we there yet?"

"We just landed." Stevie stood up and reached to retrieve their bags from the overhead compartment. "You really conked out for a while there. Must have been all those peanuts you ate after we boarded." She dropped her overstuffed backpack onto the seat with a thump.

Carole gasped at the sudden impact, which made her own seat jump a little. "Don't do that!"

Stevie paused and cocked her head to one side, giving Carole a surprised look. "What's the matter with you?"

"I had the weirdest dream just now." As the two girls shuffled out of the plane with the rest of the passengers, Carole quickly told Stevie

67

about her nightmare. When she finished, Stevie snorted.

"You should have known it was a dream all along," she pointed out. "Since when do I use words like *neat*?"

Carole shrugged and yawned. "Good point."

When the two girls stepped off the ramp into the terminal building, they both spotted a very familiar figure grinning and waving and hurrying toward them.

"Lisa!" they cried in unison.

The next few moments were lost in a flurry of hugs and exclamations. Finally Stevie pulled back and took a good, long look at Lisa.

"It's so great to see you again," she said. "You look fantastic. You're so tan!"

Lisa grinned. "Mom will probably have a cow—she sent me out here with a vat of SPF forty-five," she said. "But when you spend so much time outdoors in this incredible weather, you're bound to get a little color no matter what you do."

"I know what you mean," Stevie said. "I've been outside a lot this summer, too."

"Sure." Lisa shrugged. "But you know what they say about that California sunshine."

Stevie couldn't help frowning a little. "No, what do they say?"

Carole spoke up before Lisa could respond.

"Lisa! Your hair. It looks amazing! Did you get it cut at a fancy Hollywood salon, or what?"

Now that she took a second look, Stevie saw that Lisa's hairstyle was slightly different. At first she had assumed it was just pulled back or something, but actually it had been cut in a subtle, elegant style that framed Lisa's face, bringing out her high cheekbones and large, luminous eyes. That reminded Stevie of her last conversation with Alex before leaving home. He hadn't exactly come right out and asked her to check up on Lisa for him, but Stevie knew that was what he was thinking. Alex thought Lisa was the most beautiful girl in the world, and he was convinced that every guy who saw her would want to steal her away from him. Now that she was face-to-face with her, Stevie thought he might be on to something. She had almost forgotten how truly lovely her friend was.

"Do you like it?" Lisa put a hand to her head self-consciously, but she looked pleased, too. "Evelyn's stylist did it. Evelyn thought it would make me look, you know, a little older. More sophisticated."

Carole nodded enthusiastically. "It definitely does. I'm surprised they haven't asked you to be in that TV show yet, instead of just working behind the scenes."

Lisa laughed, looking embarrassed. "Not a

69

chance," she assured her friends. "My acting days are long behind me." She grabbed one of Carole's carry-on bags and gestured toward the baggage carousel. Her friends followed. "Besides, there's a lot more going on behind the scenes than you could ever guess. It's really fascinating, actually."

Stevie was still looking Lisa over. Besides the tan and the new hairstyle, there was something else different about her. "What's up with those clothes?" she asked abruptly. "Back home we don't dress up in our Sunday best to go to the airport."

Lisa looked surprised. She glanced down at her outfit, which consisted of a short, filmy printed skirt and a sleeveless white linen blouse. "Oh, this is no big deal. It's just an outfit Evelyn helped me pick out." She grinned. "Actually, we got it at the Galleria—you know, that famous shopping mall out here. Don't you like it?"

"Sure," Stevie said quickly. "I bet Alex would really love it, too."

"It looks great," Carole assured her, shooting Stevie a perplexed look.

Stevie shrugged, then hurried toward the baggage carousel to hide her whirl of emotions. What was wrong with her? Obviously she should have followed Carole's example and gotten some sleep on the plane. She must be overtired from the long flight—why else would she have such conflicting feelings about being here, seeing Lisa . . . *So Lisa's made a few changes to her appearance,* she told herself. *So what? She's the same person inside, right? Your best friend. So chill out and relax, okay? This trip won't do much good if you forget about one set of problems just in time to make up another whole batch to worry about.*

It didn't take long for the girls' bags to appear on the revolving baggage conveyor. "There's yours, Carole." Stevie pointed as a red nylon bag slid down the chute.

Carole nodded. She leaped forward to grab it, but she missed the handle and the bag hit the metal edge of the carousel with a resounding thud. Noticing that Carole winced at the impact, Stevie quickly guessed why.

"You're not still jumpy about that dream, are you?" she teased, hoping to lighten the mood—and to take her mind off her own brooding thoughts.

"What dream?" Lisa asked.

Looking sheepish, Carole told Lisa about it. When she finished, Lisa was smiling. "Don't worry," she told Carole as the three girls gathered up their bags and headed for the door. "Like I told you, tremors are pretty much a way of life here. Anyway, despite what people in other parts of the country think, we don't get that many of them. I seriously doubt you'll have to worry about it." She paused. "Now, as for your dream description of my dad's house . . ."

A few minutes later, Lisa was expertly steering her small red car in and out among the streams of traffic speeding by as they headed away from the airport. The road was so busy that Stevie couldn't even manage to get an accurate count of the number of lanes going in each direction.

"Let me guess," she said grimly, gripping the armrest in the backseat. Another side effect of the accident was that Stevie still felt an occasional twinge of nervousness whenever she was in a car. But she was pretty sure this traffic would have made her anxious anyway. "This must be one of those L.A. freeways you're always hearing about."

Lisa glanced at her in the rearview mirror. "Yep," she confirmed. "It was pretty nerve-racking driving here at first, especially after all those nice, peaceful country roads back home."

The words were innocent, but for some reason they rubbed Stevie the wrong way. "Oh, come on," she said. "You make Willow Creek sound like some kind of sleepy hick backwater."

Carole couldn't help noticing the tension in Stevie's voice. But she was too busy with her own worries to try to figure out what was going on with her friend. Despite Lisa's reassuring words, she couldn't stop thinking about her dream. That earthquake had felt so real . . . Carole knew that its veracity had probably been due to the jolts and shifts of the plane as it landed. Her subconscious mind had simply turned the motion of the landing into the feel of the earth shifting in a tremor—just the way she so often found herself dreaming about the school bell or a train whistle or whatever just as her alarm clock went off.

Forget the stupid dream, she advised herself sternly. *You can't enjoy all that Hollywood glitz you've been looking forward to unless you relax and stop expecting the Big One to hit at any second.* Still, she couldn't quite put it out of her mind.

At that moment she felt a rumbling and heard a loud roaring surrounding the car. She gasped and jumped but caught herself after a split second as a giant tractor trailer thundered past. Feeling her face turning red, she glanced at her friends. Luckily they hadn't noticed.

Get a grip, Carole! she told herself, sinking down in her seat and sighing.

She tried to forget about her dream by tuning back in to her friends' conversation. They were talking about Alex.

"You should see him," Stevie bragged. "He's totally buff from pushing all those lawn mowers

73

around this summer. Tan, too. I think the sun even lightened his hair a little."

"Does he talk about me?" Lisa asked, sounding wistful.

Stevie snorted. "Only every second he's awake. He's driving us all crazy. Chad can't wait to escape to his dorm next week so that he doesn't have to listen to it anymore. Michael tried to wear his portable CD player to the dinner table a few times, but Mom and Dad made him take off the earphones."

Lisa laughed. "Sounds like things haven't changed much back home."

"One thing has been totally different," Carole said. "You're not there."

Lisa smiled, looking a bit uncomfortable. Then she changed the subject and started talking about Lily. "You guys are going to love her," she said enthusiastically. "She's so adorable. I think she already looks a lot like Evelyn, but Evelyn insists she has the exact same eyes as me."

Stevie did her best to smile. "Really?" she said. "That reminds me. Max and Deborah were just saying the other day that Maxi has the same eyes as Mrs. Reg." Maxi, short for Maxine, was the elder of Max's two daughters. Most people around Pine Hollow agreed that the little girl bore a strong resemblance to Max's wife, Deborah. But there was also a definite touch of the

Regnery side of the family, particularly of Max's mother, known as Mrs. Reg.

"Oh, I haven't even asked about Max and his family yet!" Lisa cried. "How are they?"

Stevie smiled, slightly mollified. *It's about time she asked about the people back home,* she thought as she began to chatter about the Regnery family. *It's not like Alex and Carole and I are the only connections she has in Willow Creek.*

"Prancer is fine, too," Carole broke in after a few minutes. "She misses you, though."

"Really?" Lisa smiled and glanced over at her. "How can you tell?"

Carole pretended to look surprised. "She told me so, of course."

All three girls laughed, and for a moment Stevie relaxed. This was just like old times—the three best friends together, laughing and talking about horses.

Then Lisa muttered something under her breath and honked her horn—another motorist had cut too close in front of her—and the moment was shattered.

"Don't worry, we're almost there," Lisa assured her friends. She hit her turn signal and prepared to follow a line of cars heading for an exit ramp. "I know the freeways can be kind of scary if you're not used to them, but once you've been here a while they seem like a lifeline." She grinned. "You know how people say that nobody walks in L.A.? It's true."

Stevie found herself frowning again. Lisa wasn't talking like a girl who was getting ready to leave behind a strange, stressful new place and return home. She sounded more like a content, settled native who was perfectly comfortable in her surroundings. *Don't be an idiot,* she told herself sharply. *Alex's paranoia about all those hot California hunks he thinks Lisa is dating must have poisoned your brain. She's just being Lisa—making the best of the situation.*

That thought comforted her a little. But as Lisa steered the car down a wide, sunny boulevard lined with palm trees, riotous tropical-looking flowers, and stucco bungalows, she couldn't help wondering what everybody thought was so great about California. It didn't seem all that special to her.

"We've heard so much about you two! Haven't we, Lily?" Evelyn balanced the plump, giggling baby on one hip as she held out a hand to Carole and Stevie.

Carole returned the woman's open, welcoming smile. She liked her immediately. Now she saw why Lisa had adjusted so quickly to her father's new wife. Who wouldn't want a stepmother like Evelyn?

76

Mr. Atwood hadn't come home from work yet, but Evelyn and baby Lily had been waiting at the door to welcome the girls and help carry their bags to the tiny but comfortable guest room over the one-car garage. As Lisa had said, the house bore no resemblance to the sleek, modern beachside monstrosity from Carole's dream. It was a modest, pretty cottage on a quiet residential street across from a small, grassy park. The ocean was nowhere in sight, though Lisa assured them that it was just a short walk or bike ride away. The house was decorated in a quirky, homey, sunny style that seemed exactly right as soon as the girls met Evelyn.

"We've heard a lot about the two of you, too," Carole replied politely. "Haven't we, Stevie?"

"Hmmm?" Stevie had been staring around distractedly at the bright, slightly cluttered living room. It was clear she hadn't heard a word Carole had said. "Oh, um—sure."

Carole didn't want Evelyn to think they were being rude, so she spoke quickly to cover Stevie's confusion. "May I hold Lily?" she asked.

Evelyn looked pleased. "Of course you may, Carole. Here you go. I just changed her diaper, so you shouldn't have to worry about any leaks."

Carole giggled and reached for the baby. Soon Lily was snuggled into her arms, gazing up with wide, innocent blue eyes. "Aren't you the cutest little—" Carole cut off her cooing words with a gasp. "What was that?" she cried. This time she knew she wasn't imagining it, and she knew it wasn't a truck. The floor was shaking—just slightly, but definitely shaking. She clutched the baby to her chest so tightly that Lily began to squirm.

"It's okay, Carole," Evelyn assured her quickly. "It's just a tremor. It will be over in a second."

Sure enough, the shaking ceased almost as soon as the words were out of Evelyn's mouth. But Carole was still trembling. She quickly handed Lily to Lisa, then sank down into a nearby chair, feeling slightly faint. "Wow," she said.

"Hey, that was weird!" Stevie exclaimed. She looked nervous, too, though not nearly as terrified as Carole felt. "How do you people live like that? I mean, back home we get the occasional bad thunderstorm or something, but this . . ."

Evelyn laughed gently, shooting Carole a concerned look. "It doesn't seem that weird if you've grown up here, like I have," she explained.

"And even if you haven't, you can get used to it," Lisa put in. "It's not so bad, really. At first I was sure every tremor meant the Big One was coming, but now I hardly notice them."

"Really?" Stevie cocked a disbelieving eyebrow at her friend.

Lisa grinned. "Okay, I admit it. I still notice them. But they don't bother me much anymore. Honestly."

Carole wasn't entirely convinced. "I don't know about this," she said shakily. "There was a tremor the other night when we were on the phone, and now this. Maybe they're leading up to something more serious." She glanced at her watch, suddenly wishing they could just get back in the car and return to the airport for the next flight back to Virginia. *There might not be any movie stars there,* she thought, *or much glamour, either. But at least the ground isn't always shifting under your feet!*

FIVE

"This is great." Carole leaned back in her wicker chair with a sigh. "But I'm so stuffed, I don't think I'll ever eat again."

"Does that mean you've decided to stick around for a few days and risk the Big One?" Lisa teased.

Carole stuck out her tongue playfully. "Very funny," she said. "Don't you know you shouldn't make fun of other people's phobias?" Still, she had to admit that she was feeling a lot more relaxed today, after a full—and tremor-free—day exploring Southern California with Lisa and Stevie.

At the moment, the three girls were relaxing on the broad cedar deck of a bistro overlooking the Pacific Ocean, enjoying the warm evening breezes and digesting a meal of fresh fruits and vegetables and even fresher seafood. They had worked up a hearty appetite exploring the sights that day, from the hustle and bustle of downtown Hollywood to the luxurious mansions in Beverly Hills.

"It's too bad we didn't have time to hit Universal Studios today," Stevie said, taking a sip of her iced tea. "I heard that *Jaws* ride they have is pretty cool."

Carole was glad to see that some of the prickliness she'd sensed in Stevie the day before seemed to have worn off. *Maybe she's finally relaxing and putting the accident and everything else back home out of her mind,* she thought with relief. *I hope so. She deserves a break from all that.* Carole herself was more than ready to forget about earthquakes and other unpleasant things as much as possible and enjoy every moment she had to spend in California. Sitting there gazing at the cool blue water of the Pacific, the world of whiny riding students, sweaty tack, and manure-filled stalls seemed very far away.

She nodded in response to Stevie's comment. "Maybe we can do that tomorrow. I'm also dying to get a look at Rodeo Drive. Normally I'm not much of a shopper, but I've seen it on TV and in the movies so many times that I feel like I should check it out, you know?"

Stevie nodded. "Me too. Maybe if we get started early tomorrow we can do Rodeo Drive and Universal Studios and then take a ride up the coast in the evening. I've heard the scenery north of here is awesome."

"Sounds good," Carole said. "How far is San Diego from here, by the way? I wouldn't mind going to the zoo there if . . ." Suddenly Carole noticed that Lisa was frowning a little. "What's wrong?"

"There's no way we'll be able to fit in all that stuff in one day," Lisa said. "I have a job, remember? My boss gave me the day off because it was your first day here, but he's expecting me bright and early tomorrow morning. We're shooting some complicated scenes with the horses, and he'll need me."

"Oh, right. Your job." Stevie had almost forgotten about Lisa's summer job with Skye's TV show. Now that Lisa had reminded her, she was a little surprised that she hadn't taken off the whole week so that she could spend more time with them. After all, the summer was almost over. Stevie had quit her own job at a local laundry as soon as she'd found out about this trip.

Still, she guessed she couldn't blame her friend for wanting to stick it out as long as possible. Lisa had a lot more interesting stuff to stare at all day than washing machines and detergent—stuff like incredible-looking TV stars and purebred horses.

Carole was thinking along much the same

lines. It was no surprise that Lisa wanted to squeeze every last drop of excitement out of her taste of show business. Beautiful horses, good-looking actors—what could be better? It sounded sort of like what Carole's own job at Pine Hollow might be if, instead of sniffly preteens, the riders were all gorgeous, talented twenty-year-old hunks. "I guess you wouldn't want to miss out on one extra minute of that job, right? I'm surprised you could stand to stay away today."

Lisa felt her jaw clenching tightly as she wondered just exactly what Carole meant by that. And what had that odd expression been in Stevie's eyes as she'd said your *job*? Despite the balmy, peaceful surroundings and the memory of a fun-filled day, Lisa was starting to feel a twinge of annoyance with her two best friends. She was proud of her work on the set this summer—her *hard* work—and she had hoped to be able to share those feelings with them. But it was becoming painfully obvious that they didn't take her commitment to her job very seriously.

They're probably picturing me lounging around by a pool somewhere, chatting on a cell phone and sipping fruit smoothies with a bunch of glamorous stars, she thought sourly. Then she caught herself. She was being unfair, even if she didn't like to admit it. Her friends knew very well how much hard work it was taking care of horses. They were just a bit overwhelmed by the thought of good-looking TV stars and capricious Hollywood moguls, much as Lisa had been when she had first arrived. That was probably why they were talking as though Lisa's job was about as serious as a trip to Disneyland.

Don't tell them, show them. Lisa could almost hear Evelyn's voice as she thought about her stepmother's favorite saying. In this case, it was the perfect solution.

"Listen," she said, forcing herself to relax and smile at her friends. "I've got an idea. Why don't you guys come to work with me tomorrow? I'm sure it will be okay. There are going to be all sorts of extra people hanging around the set anyway—some magazine is coming to shoot a spread for their next issue."

"Really?" Carole grinned. "Cool! Just in case watching them film a TV show isn't amazing enough, now we get to check out a real Hollywood photo shoot, too!" She sighed. "You're lucky, Lisa. You must have had an incredible summer working there."

Stevie sat up straight. "That does sound pretty cool," she admitted. "Now if I have to do one of Miss Fenton's famous 'What I Did This Summer' essays at school, I'll have something more interesting to write about than watching a bunch

of strangers' socks whirling around in the dryer."
She leaned over and gave Lisa a gentle punch on
the arm. "Seriously, though. Great idea, Lisa.
Thanks for inviting us."

Their enthusiasm made Lisa feel a little bit
better. *See? They're just excited about all this Hol-*
lywood stuff, she thought. *When they see that I'm*
really just working in a stable, they'll understand
that this is a serious job like any other.

Still, as she gazed at her friends across the table, she couldn't help thinking how strange it
was to see them sitting there in her favorite bistro, overlooking one of her favorite views of the
now-familiar Pacific shoreline. They didn't belong in this world, and a part of Lisa's mind
couldn't seem to reconcile their presence.

Another part of her, though, was simply
overjoyed to have her best friends with her again.
She had missed them in the past months, but she
hadn't realized quite how much until she had
seen them in the flesh. She had never been apart
from them for so long, not since they had all
met. And despite the separation, despite her own
conflicted feelings, being with them now still
gave her a feeling unlike any other, a sense of
being an important part of something larger
than herself, of being complete.

Well, almost complete, Lisa reminded herself.
The person who really gave her that one-of-a-

kind feeling of wholeness, deep down in her soul, was Alex. Seeing her friends from Willow Creek made her constant sense of missing him shift from a deep, gentle ache into something sharper and almost unbearable. At moments she thought she couldn't wait one more minute— that she had to see him, touch him, kiss him right then and there or she would go crazy.

I shouldn't be thinking that way, she chided herself. *The summer's almost over, and soon we'll be together again. All of us.*

That thought made her feel sad, just for a moment. Leaving here didn't only mean going back home again to all the people, places, horses, and other things she missed there. It meant starting to miss a whole new set of people, places, and horses she would be leaving behind in California.

Carole spoke up. "Should we get going? It's almost nine, and you promised we could take a walk on the beach before it gets totally dark."

"Oh!" Lisa glanced at her watch. Nine o'clock was a very special time for her these days. It was the hour she and Alex had agreed upon when each of them would look up at the night sky and think of the other.

The three girls left the restaurant and walked down to the beach. Lisa dropped a few steps behind her friends and sought out the moon, shining clearly in the darkening sky. Somewhere, far far away, she knew that Alex was staring at the same moon and thinking of her. It was midnight in Willow Creek, so he was probably in his room, exhausted after a long day of mowing lawns. She tried to picture him sitting at his window, his gentle, caring eyes focused upward. The image made her smile, and she felt another pang of that intense longing to see him, the strongest one yet.

"Soon," she whispered quietly enough so that Carole and Stevie wouldn't hear. "We'll be together again soon."

Then she sighed. Yes, she would be with Alex soon, and that particular ache in her heart would be eased at last.

But it would be replaced by others. The ache of being separated from her father. Of not getting to watch Lily continue to grow up; of leaving behind the little sister she had come to love so deeply. Of missing other friends new and old, from Evelyn and Skye to other friends at work. Even the horses on the set had become special to her in their own lovable, quirky, interesting ways.

Why does my life have to be split in two? Lisa wondered desperately, not for the first time. *Why do the two halves have to be so far apart?*

She gazed at her best friends as they wandered

ahead down the beach. Carole was casting slightly nervous glances at a section of rocky cliff just above where they were walking, probably worrying what would happen if an earthquake struck. Stevie was watching a bird land on the sand nearby, probably comparing it—unfavorably—to the birds back home in Willow Creek.

Lisa sighed. *And how can I love two completely different lives so much when they hardly overlap at all—and probably never will?*

SIX

". . . and this is Skye's horse, Topsy." Lisa
stopped in front of a spacious box stall and patted the curious bay gelding. Topsy immediately
stuck his head out to see who they were. "He
reminds me a little of Belle, Stevie. He's fun-
loving and spirited and a real sweetheart."

"True. The only problem is, like all the horses
around this place, he likes Lisa better than he
likes me," Skye joked.

Stevie chuckled along with the others, but her
eyes narrowed as she reached out to give the
friendly bay a pat. She had been watching Skye
closely ever since he had greeted the three girls
on the set a few minutes before. It had started
out as more of a formality than anything else.
Stevie had promised Alex she would look after
his interests, and she was a loyal sister.

But then she had laid eyes on Skye. Stevie
hadn't seen him in person in a couple of years,
and she had to admit that he was the same old

89

Skye, friendly, funny, unassuming—and good-looking. Very, very good-looking. Somehow, when they had all been younger, Skye's looks hadn't seemed that important. But now she had to admit that she was starting to understand, at least a little, what Alex was so worried about. Not that Lisa couldn't be trusted to control herself, but still, she had always been closer to Skye than Stevie or Carole, and it seemed that their friendship had flourished over the summer.

Key word: friendship, Stevie reminded herself. *If Lisa hasn't fallen for Skye up until now, there's no reason it should happen this summer. Right?*

As the group continued slowly down the row of stalls, admiring the inhabitants, Carole wasn't thinking about Lisa's relationship with Skye at all. She was too busy enjoying what she had come for: glamour, horses, and more glamour. On their way over from the parking lot she had caught a glimpse of Skye's good-looking costar, Jeremiah Jamison. She had learned from Skye that a couple of other famous actors would be on the set that day shooting guest appearances on the series. Now Skye and Lisa were giving Carole and Stevie the grand tour, showing them some of what went on behind the scenes, introducing them to all sorts of people, from Lisa's boss, Rick, to the director of the show. It was incredible.

The stables were pretty incredible, too. Carole didn't think she had ever seen so many stunning, perfectly groomed horses in one spot before. It all helped her to forget that the ground might start shaking beneath her feet again at any moment. . . .

"So Skye," she said brightly, determined not to think about earthquakes anymore, "we're dying to hear more about the show. Lisa's hardly told us anything."

"Not true," Lisa protested. "I told you it's called *Paradise Ranch,* and Skye plays Devon Drake, the hunky son of the ranch owners. Practically every female who comes near the ranch falls madly in love with him, but he's loyal to his one true love." She paused and gave a mischievous wink. "His horse."

"Very funny." Skye shoved her playfully, then turned to the other girls. "Actually, I'm a soul-searching young man who doesn't know what he wants out of life." He shrugged. "At least that's what the director keeps saying. I think he's trying to tantalize me with the prospect of some heavy acting scenes later in the season so I won't complain about having to kiss all those beautiful guest stars all the time."

Carole rolled her eyes. "Sounds like torture."

Skye just grinned. "Anyway, the concept of the show is pretty simple. Drake, his parents,

91

and his sister—who's played by Summer Kirke, you've probably seen her in the movies—are struggling to keep the ranch going despite the best efforts of the rival Torrence clan. They own a development company that wants to buy up the land."

"There are a few other continuing characters, too," Lisa went on. "Like the crazy hermit who lives on the ranch, and a couple of ranch hands, and Devon's best friend Rand Hayden—"

"Jeremiah Jamison plays him, right?" Carole asked eagerly. "I saw an article about him in a magazine last week and they mentioned the show."

Skye nodded. "I'm not surprised. Jeremiah's got a killer publicist. Yes, he plays Rand, who's sort of the main good guy besides my character."

"In addition to the main characters, there are always lots of guest stars playing the guests who come and stay at the ranch." Lisa stopped in front of the last stall in the shed row, where a dainty Arabian mare was looking over the half door. "This is Fancy," she said. "She's the horse Summer rides."

"Right," said a deep voice from behind them. "And Summer's got to ride her in the rattlesnake scene today, and Fancy can't groom or saddle herself."

Turning, Carole saw Rick standing across the way with his hands on his hips.

"Aye, aye, sir," Lisa called, giving him a snappy mock salute. "I'll have her ready in no time."

Rick nodded gruffly and strode off.

"Talk about double vision," Stevie whispered as Rick disappeared around the corner of the shed row. "For a second there, I thought Max had stowed away with us!"

Lisa giggled. "I'd better get to work," she said. "Much like Max, when Rick gives an order, he means business."

"Can we help?" Carole volunteered.

"You don't have to ask twice," Lisa said quickly. "This is a stable, after all. And you know what that means."

Stevie let out a mock groan. "Plenty of work for everyone!"

Stevie was grooming a placid gray gelding when Lisa turned up at the door to the stall, looking harried. "Someone needs to warm up Fancy now, but I'm supposed to be getting the tack ready for today's shoot. Can you help me out?"

"You can count on me," Stevie replied immediately, tossing the currycomb she was using back in the trunk outside the stall door. She

93

never would have believed it, but the stable chores she'd been doing had made her feel better than anything else on this trip so far. It was wonderful to be in a stable without worrying that Callie and Scott might come in at any moment and remind her of—Stevie shook her head. She wasn't going to think about any of that. "What do you want me to do?" she asked Lisa. "Tack or warm-up?"

"Warm-up." Lisa was already leading the way toward Fancy's stall. "She's all groomed and saddled and everything. You just need to get her loosened up. Summer should be showing up soon to run through her scene. She's a little nervous about it and she wants to get in some serious practice."

"The rattlesnake scene, right? I'd be nervous, too."

Lisa grinned. "Actually, there's no real rattlesnake," she explained. "That'll be added later by the special effects people. But Fancy—and Summer, of course—will have to act like the snake is right there in front of them."

Stevie wrinkled her forehead in confusion. "How are they going to do that?" She shrugged. "I mean, Summer can just pretend or whatever, but how do you get a horse to fake something like that?"

"It's really amazing," Lisa said as she swung

open the door to Fancy's stall. As promised, the pretty chestnut was saddled and waiting inside. Lisa unfastened the mare's lead rope and led her outside and down the aisle as Stevie followed. "You may think these horses were all chosen just for their good looks, but actually most of them are trained to within an inch of their lives. Fancy can do all sorts of tricks, including rearing on command and tossing her head with her ears back."

"Cool!" Stevie looked at the dainty Arabian with new respect. "Do I get to try that?"

Lisa hesitated, then shrugged. "Why not?" she said. "Rick ran her through the motions a couple of days ago, but it couldn't hurt to make sure she remembers." She quickly explained the commands that would make the mare do the trick. "Just be careful, okay?"

"Aren't I always?" Stevie replied, taking the reins from Lisa and giving Fancy a pat on the neck.

"No," Lisa said with a grin. "That's why I said it. I've got to go. I'll try to be back before Summer gets here, but if she shows up, stick around in case she needs any help, okay? Good luck!"

"Thanks." Stevie led the mare toward the dusty practice ring beyond the last shed row. She mounted, then spent a few minutes riding around the ring slowly, getting to know the horse. Lisa had been right to say that Fancy was well trained. Stevie hardly had to give a command before the mare had executed it. When she was confident that the two of them were communicating well, she asked the mare to trot, then canter. Fancy switched leads on signal, shortening and lengthening her stride as soon as Stevie asked.

Finally Stevie was convinced that Fancy was warmed up sufficiently. She took a deep breath. It was time to try the rearing command.

"Just call me Stevie Lake, Hollywood stunt rider," she murmured. Fancy's dainty ears flicked back at the sound of her rider's voice, then forward again alertly.

Stevie drew her to a stop in the center of the ring. She tried to imagine how an actress like Summer Kirke would mentally prepare for this scene. Perhaps she would close her eyes for a moment and imagine the horrible snake on the ground below. Or maybe she would draw on some fearful experience in her own past to create the proper look of terror.

"Whatever," Stevie said aloud. She didn't have to act out the scene. All she had to do was make sure the horse could do her part when the time came.

She settled herself more firmly in the saddle,

then gave the signal. As usual, Fancy responded instantly, letting out a loud, sharp whinny and then rising quickly onto her hind legs, her forelegs flailing in the air in front of her as she tossed her head.

"*Yeeeee-ha!*" Stevie cried gleefully. Under normal circumstances a rearing horse was a scary thing because it meant the rider had lost control. But Stevie knew that Fancy was still very much under her control. The mare wasn't about to race off or start bucking, trying to unseat her. She wouldn't rear back so far that she toppled over backward, crushing her. No—Fancy was *acting*, or at least coming as close to it as an animal could come. And it was fun!

When Fancy's front hooves hit the ground again, Stevie gave the command once more, enjoying the ride. Then she let the horse settle down for good, giving her an appreciative pat.

"That was fantastic, girl," she said. "Thanks. Now come on, we'd better quit or you'll be too tired for your real rider."

She turned the horse and headed for the gate. She noticed a young woman standing just outside the ring, her hands clutched tightly at her sides.

Stevie's eyes widened. She recognized Summer Kirke right away. The actress was even more beautiful in person than she looked on the movie screen.

"Hi!" Stevie called, urging Fancy toward her. "My name's Stevie Lake, and I—"

"You don't have to introduce yourself to me." As Stevie got closer, she could see that Summer's face was pale and upset. "It's obvious who you are."

"Huh?" Stevie stopped just inside the gate and slid out of the saddle.

Summer tossed her head, sending her wavy blond hair sliding back over her slender shoulders. Absently, Stevie noticed that the highlights in the star's hair were the exact shade of Fancy's mane. "I should have known they'd replace me. I could tell from the start that Rick didn't think I rode well enough. And you and Fancy certainly seem to get along."

Stevie was starting to feel very confused. What was Summer talking about? Why would she think she was being replaced just because Stevie was riding her horse? "You don't understand," she protested.

"I understand plenty." Summer's face crumpled suddenly, and tears started to run down her flawless cheeks. Before Stevie could speak, the actress buried her face in her hands and started sobbing as if her heart would break.

Stevie had never felt so awkward in her life.

She looked around desperately for help. Luckily it was heading her way from the shed row at that very moment, in the form of Lisa Atwood. Carole was at Lisa's heels.

"What's going on?" Lisa asked breathlessly, rushing up to them. "Summer, what's wrong?"

"She just started crying," Stevie said helplessly. "I don't know what happened. I didn't do anything."

Summer raised her tear-streaked face to look at Lisa, and Carole almost gasped aloud. Even in her present state, the young actress was breathtaking. Carole had seen Summer Kirke in the movies, but in real life her beauty was even more astonishing. What could anyone who looked like that possibly have to cry about?

Lisa had her arm around Summer's shoulders and was making soothing noises. "It's okay, Summer," she crooned. "Tell me what's wrong, okay?"

Summer took a deep, shuddery breath and managed to stop crying. "I'm being replaced," she said in a shaky voice. "Why didn't you tell me, Lisa? You must have known. It's because I can't ride that well, isn't it?"

"Don't be silly! You're a terrific rider," Lisa said, a look of understanding dawning on her face. "And they'd never replace you. You're one of the stars of the show!"

Summer glanced over at Stevie with a frown. "Then what's she doing here?" she said. "Is she a stunt double? I told the director I'd practice the scene until I could do it, but I guess he didn't believe me."

Lisa was already shaking her head. "She's not a stunt double, either," she assured Summer. "She was just warming up Fancy so she'd be nice and limber when you got here."

Summer didn't look convinced. She looked at Stevie again. "But she's got my coloring, and we're about the same height . . ." She bit her lip. "I see her exercising my horse—what am I supposed to think?"

"I'm so sorry about the confusion," Lisa said reassuringly. "Actually, Summer, this is my friend Stevie. She's just visiting for the day, and I asked her to help out with Fancy. I should have introduced you earlier."

"Oh." Finally Summer looked mollified. A small, slightly embarrassed smile played over her full lips. "She's a friend of yours?"

"That's right."

Carole heaved a sigh of relief as Lisa explained their presence to Summer. Lisa had managed to defuse an explosive situation. She was impressed. It seemed there was more to this job than just stable chores.

For a moment she wondered why on earth

Summer had jumped to such a silly conclusion about Stevie, even if their hair *was* approximately the same shade. It didn't make much sense.

But she forgot all about that question as Lisa introduced her and Summer reached for her hand. *I'm shaking hands with a real movie star!* Carole thought gleefully. *If only those bratty Pony Clubbers could see me now!*

This was just the kind of showbiz experience she'd been hoping for. It would make a fantastic story to think about back at Pine Hollow when she was mucking out stalls and figuring out feeding schedules.

She pushed those thoughts out of her mind. She wasn't going to think about her chores back home until she had to, and in the meantime, she was determined to squeeze every ounce of glamour and excitement she could out of this trip.

At least until the Big One hit.

SEVEN

"Ready for a break? They're about to do a run-through of this afternoon's scene and I thought you might want to watch."

"We are *so* there!" Stevie jumped up quickly from her seat on the floor of the tack room, where she was polishing a handful of bits.

Carole got up, too. "Is this that rattlesnake scene?"

Lisa shook her head. "Summer's the only one in that scene, and she likes to avoid public run-throughs whenever she can," she explained. "The scene they're doing now is actually one of Skye's big romantic encounters." She winked drolly. "He's been moaning and groaning about it all morning, but when I stopped by his trailer a few minutes ago he was brushing his teeth like there's no tomorrow."

Stevie felt that now familiar twinge of concern. What was Lisa doing stopping by Skye's trailer? She was a stable hand—she was supposed to work with horses, not people. Especially not incredibly good-looking male people.

"Are there any horses in this scene?" Carole asked.

Lisa grinned. "Glad you asked. I'm supposed to bring them out right now. Any volunteers to help me?"

Soon the three girls and Rick were leading out four tacked-up horses, including Skye's mount, Topsy. Lisa went first, heading to the set for the remote camping spot where romantic young Devon Drake liked to take his love interests. It consisted of a ring of rocks around a fire pit, with a couple of large logs and boulders scattered nearby to serve as seating. Wildflowers peeked out of the grassy lawn, and a thickly forested rocky slope formed a backdrop. It would be a pretty romantic spot, Stevie guessed, if it weren't for the semicircle of huge cameras and lights that stood just a few feet away. Not to mention the crowd of people milling around, shouting directions at one another and generally causing a racket. Rick immediately broke off from the rest of them in search of Jeremiah Jamison, whose horse he was leading.

Stevie glanced over her shoulder at Topsy, who was following her calmly toward the chaotic scene. "I guess you're used to this, huh, boy?" She couldn't help thinking that the hot, noisy, dusty set was an unnatural place for horses—not like the calm, quiet fields and shady paddocks of Pine Hollow.

Skye had just spotted her and was hurrying over. He was in full makeup and dressed in an outfit that could only be his show costume—leather chaps and a Western shirt unbuttoned halfway down his muscular chest.

She did her best not to smirk. "Looking good, Skye," she said. "Maybe after work you can give me some makeup tips. I've been searching for a new mascara. . . ."

Carole, who had just walked up with a huge but rather timid black gelding in tow, rolled her eyes. "Don't listen to her, Skye. She just doesn't understand the world of show business." She paused. "Actually, though, I thought this was a run-through. Isn't that like a rehearsal? They're not taping it, are they?"

"Nope," Skye replied, straight-faced. "You found me out. I just love wearing makeup. Actually, I'm in talks with Natural Beauty to be their new spokesmodel."

"Stop it, Skye." Lisa laughed. She had arrived just in time to hear him and halted the chestnut gelding she was leading to explain. "Check out that woman over there—in the light blue suit, see her? She's a reporter from that new entertainment magazine, *Star Struck,* and the skinny guy next to her is her photographer."

"Oh! I get it. They're doing an article about the show. That's why everybody's made up." Carole craned her neck for a better look. This was so exciting she could hardly stand it. She had never thought of herself as a Hollywood groupie—she had always been too busy with horses for that—but now that she was here, she had to admit that it was just as exciting as she had hoped. *Definitely the break I needed from the daily grind,* she thought with a smile. She loved Pine Hollow, but it was hardly glamorous, especially when she was carting a load of manure to the manure pit or shoving medication down a recalcitrant horse's slimy throat.

"I'll be right back. I want to introduce today's love interest to her horse." Lisa nodded toward Skye's pretty young female guest star, a perky, dark-haired actress Carole recognized from a different TV show. "You guys wait here. Matthew will come for his horse when he's ready." She nodded at the big black gelding.

Carole was looking in the other direction. "Wow. Who's *he*?"

Lisa turned to see. "Oh, that's him. Matthew Reeves. I forgot you hadn't met him yet. He's the actor who plays Nick Torrence, the son of the rival family that's out to ruin the Drakes."

As Lisa headed off with the chestnut gelding, Carole managed to tear her eyes away from the incredible-looking young actor. She didn't want to miss anything interesting by spending all her time goggling over cute guys, as tempting as it was. "This is amazing," she told Stevie and Skye. "I never realized it took so many people to make one TV show. I mean, I know we've watched some of your shoots before, Skye, but it's been a while. Anyway, those weren't right here in Hollywood."

"Pretty wild, huh?" Skye smiled. "If you want to see something really entertaining, watch the director." He pointed out a short man with receding brown hair and a neatly trimmed beard. "We're all convinced he's afraid of horses, but he won't admit it."

Stevie giggled. "You're kidding. This guy is directing a show that takes place on a ranch and he's afraid of horses?"

"That's kind of sad, really. Especially if he won't let anyone help him." Carole wasn't as amused by the irony of the situation as Stevie seemed to be. She couldn't imagine being afraid of horses herself, but she understood that some people got very nervous around the huge, powerful creatures. Over the years, she had helped more than one horse-phobic person get over his fears, so she knew it could be done—but only if the person was willing to work to overcome the problem.

Carole watched along with the others as the guest star chatted animatedly at the director, who was keeping a steady eye on the chestnut gelding standing calmly at the young woman's shoulder. Skye was right, Carole decided. The director looked decidedly uncomfortable, though he was standing his ground. She wondered if his fear was based on a real experience or was just a case of unfamiliarity with horses. That might make a difference in whether he eventually adjusted on his own. . . .

"Hi there," said an unfamiliar voice. "You must be new."

Carole turned—and found herself looking into the sea green eyes of Matthew Reeves. She just gaped for a second. Then, realizing that she must look like a total idiot—or, worse, a hick from Virginia goggling over everything she saw—she clamped her mouth shut firmly and forced a casual smile. "Hi yourself," she replied. "I *am* new. I mean, I'm just visiting. I mean—"

Skye came to her rescue. "This is Carole. She's a friend of Lisa's."

"Oh!" Matthew's smile broadened. "Cool. Any friend of Lisa's is a friend of mine. So is Conejo ready for his close-up?" He gestured to the horse Carole was leading.

"Conejo?" In her mind, Carole had dubbed the big black gelding Scaredy-Cat because he was so flighty and nervous—though fortunately the crowd of people all around him didn't seem to be making his state of mind any worse. "Oh, you mean this guy. I didn't know his real name." She gave the horse a pat, causing his ears to go back for a second before they swiveled toward a piece of equipment rolling by in front of him.

"Right. It's Spanish for *rabbit*," Matthew explained, reaching for the lead line as he talked. "They named him that because he's so jumpy, like a scared little bunny."

"Luckily he doesn't look that way onscreen," Skye put in with a chuckle. "It wouldn't look too good for the evil and scheming Nick Torrence to ride a wimp of a horse, eh, Matt?"

"You said it, buddy." Matthew slapped the horse fondly on the neck. "On camera, all that nervous energy comes across as fiery spirit." His face twisted suddenly into a dark scowl. The transformation was so immediate and extreme that Carole gasped involuntarily. "And that's the way Nick Torrence likes his mount. Fiery." He stalked away with the horse prancing cautiously behind him.

Carole turned to Skye, wide-eyed. "Wow," she breathed.

Stevie nodded. "Talk about Dr. Jekyll and Mr.

Hyde. Or is it Dr. Hyde and Mr. Jekyll? I can never remember."

Skye was grinning. "Matt takes his role as black-hearted bad guy pretty seriously." He glanced over the girls' heads in the direction of the director, who had finished his conversation with the guest star and was shouting out orders. "Oops, I'd better get over there. Enjoy the show, okay?" He led Topsy toward the director.

"Where should we go?" Carole glanced around uncertainly, feeling very much in the way. Everybody except her and Stevie seemed to have an important job to do.

Before Stevie could answer, Lisa came rushing toward them. "They're about to get started. Come on, we can watch from over here." She led the way to a quiet spot on a small, grassy hill off to one side with an unobstructed view of the action.

"Still think Nick Torrence is a major hunk, Carole?" Stevie whispered teasingly as the cast completed their first run-through of the scene.

Carole shuddered. "Believe me, I am *so* over him," she declared, thinking back over the action they had just witnessed.

The scene had begun with Devon Drake and his love interest getting to know each other by the campfire. However, their blissful moment had been interrupted by Nick Torrence, who had started a rockslide on the boulder-studded slope behind the campfire. Carole had winced, her mind immediately flashing back to her earthquake dream. But she had been distracted from her fears by the exciting action that followed. The gallant Devon had reacted quickly to the disaster, shielding his lady love and pushing her to safety while being overcome by the shower of stones himself. As Nick Torrence cackled gleefully in the forest, Devon's faithful friend Rand Hayden had happened by just in time to save the day by heroically dragging the unconscious Devon out of range of the battering hail of rocks.

At least that was how the scene would play out for viewers at home. In reality, it had been quite a bit slower and more complicated. The special-effects people had been the ones to set off the rockslide—Lisa assured her friends quietly that all the stones and boulders were made of papier-mâché or foam. There had been other breaks in the action, too. For instance, the makeup artists had had to rush in and add bruises and dirt to the actors' faces and bodies. Despite all the pauses, though, the scene had sped by for the fascinated Virginia visitors.

"Anyway, who needs Nick Torrence when that gorgeous Rand Hayden is around?" Carole went on with a grin. She knew she was starting to sound like a starry-eyed teenybopper, but she didn't care. She was in Hollywood—she was going to go with it. "He seems so noble and smart."

"True." Stevie nodded, clearly playing along and enjoying it. "Not like that conniving jerk Nick. Who needs that kind of trouble?"

Lisa gave her friends an uncertain glance. "You guys are just joking around, right? You know those guys are just acting. They're not really like the characters they play."

"Duh." Stevie shrugged and looked thoughtful. "Still, you have to wonder a little. My guess is that only a real creep could play a real creep so well."

"And only someone who's earnest and sensitive in real life could be so convincing as Rand," Carole went on, grasping Stevie's point immediately. It made a lot of sense when she thought about it. The casting people probably sought out actors who were similar to the characters they were supposed to play. That would make things easier for everyone, especially the actors themselves.

"Hey, you promised to introduce us to everyone, but we haven't met Jeremiah yet," Stevie reminded Lisa. "I want to be able to tell everyone at school that he's a close personal friend of mine. So how about it?"

Carole nodded eagerly. She had no plans to brag to people about her Hollywood experience, but she wanted to have plenty of stuff to look back on and daydream about during math class or marathon tack-cleaning sessions. "Come on, Lisa. It looks like they're taking a break." She gestured toward Jeremiah, who had handed his horse's reins to Rick and was strolling toward the reporter and photographer from *Star Struck*.

"I don't know if we should bother him right now." Lisa looked reluctant. "Maybe later."

"Forget later," Stevie said. "We're not planning to barge in on his interview, if that's what you're worried about. We can just hang out nearby and catch him when he's done. It'll only take a second."

"Well, I don't know." Lisa glanced toward Jeremiah, who was giving the reporter a shy, humble smile as they chatted. "He's probably got a lot on his mind right now, and we wouldn't want to distract him or anything."

Stevie gave her a searching look. What was the problem? Lisa had seemed eager enough to introduce them to just about everyone else on the set. Why not Jeremiah?

Maybe she wants him all to herself, a nasty little voice whispered inside her. *Maybe it's not Skye you should be worried about.*

"Shut up, Alex," she muttered aloud.

"What?" Carole glanced at her. "Did you say something?"

"I just said, it couldn't hurt to go down there," Stevie said quickly, waving a hand toward Jeremiah. "If he doesn't want to talk to us, he doesn't have to." Without waiting for Lisa to reply, she started down the hill.

"I'm in love," Carole declared melodramatically, almost dropping Conejo's lead line as she clasped her heart. "Call out the preacher and rent me a hall. This is it."

Stevie rolled her eyes, but she was smiling. "I don't know," she teased. "I'd swear he winked at *me*. I don't know how I'm going to break the news to Phil, though—maybe Jeremiah and I will name our firstborn son after him."

"Very funny, guys," Lisa said dryly as the three girls strolled toward the stable. The rehearsal had ended, and they were leading the tired horses back to their stalls. "You'd better watch out, Stevie, or I'll have to tell Phil you were drooling all over yourself just because a good-looking guy smiled at you."

Carole giggled. "Good. Then Phil will lock Stevie up in a tower somewhere, and Jeremiah will be all mine!" She felt a bit giddy. Jeremiah Jamison had been every bit as wonderful as the character he played. He had even excused himself from his conversation with the reporter to greet each of Lisa's friends and kiss their hands gallantly.

"Whatever." Lisa let out a snort. "Come on, let's hurry and get these horses cleaned up. They have to be well rested for this afternoon's shoot. I'll meet you in the tack room in a few, okay?" She turned and led her horse down the aisle toward its stall.

"She's so jaded," Carole whispered to Stevie jokingly. "Come on. We'd better get these guys cleaned up."

Stevie nodded agreeably. "I think they're both in the last shed row, right? Good, we can cross-tie them outside their stalls and talk about you-know-who while we— Oh, hi, Summer." The beautiful young actress had just appeared around the corner of one of the buildings in front of them.

"Hi." Summer smiled shyly at them while stepping aside to let them pass with the horses.

Carole smiled back before returning to her previous topic of conversation. "Anyway, Stevie, as your friend I want to let you know that you're insane if you think Jeremiah has any interest in you. As soon as we looked into each other's eyes, I could tell—"

"Are you talking about Jeremiah Jamison?" Summer interrupted.

Carole glanced at her in surprise. She had forgotten that the actress was still within earshot. "Oh, uh—yeah," she said, feeling embarrassed. Just because meeting Jeremiah had made her feel like a goofy, adoring kid didn't mean she wanted other people to see her acting like one. "We're just kidding around, though."

"Oh, good." Summer's cheeks had turned pink and she looked flustered. "Um, I don't want to intrude or anything. But Jeremiah, you know—well, I'm just glad. That's all." She lowered her head and hurried away, her big blue eyes blinking fast.

As soon as she was out of sight, Stevie let out a low whistle. "What was that all about?"

Carole shrugged, gazing in the direction Summer had gone. "Who knows? Lisa told us Summer's always kind of emotional."

Stevie nodded, remembering the sensitive star's tantrum earlier that day. "I didn't need any more convincing about that."

The two girls got their horses moving again. Carole's mind drifted back to Jeremiah, and she smiled dreamily. "Maybe she has a reason this time, though," she joked. "Maybe she's jealous because she thinks Jeremiah's getting more attention than she is. I've read about these superstar Hollywood egos."

"Maybe," Stevie agreed. She tugged on

Topsy's lead as the gelding tried to stop and sniff at the ground along the path. "Or maybe she has some kind of unrequited crush on Jeremiah herself. Who could blame her for that?"

"They'd make quite a couple, wouldn't they?" Carole paused and frowned. "Actually, now that I think about it, weren't they a couple once? I thought I saw a story on TV a few months ago about Summer Kirke and her gorgeous new man. I didn't know who Jeremiah Jamison was then, but it must have been him. Nobody else could be that good-looking."

"You've got me." Stevie shrugged. "Anyway, they don't seem to have anything going right now, if they ever did." She grinned wickedly. "And that means he's all mine."

Carole laughed and prepared to retaliate. *This is great,* she thought happily. *Not only do we get to visit Lisa, but we get to have the total Hollywood experience, too—wild starstruck crush and all!*

EIGHT

"Whew!" Carole paused, wiped her brow, and leaned on the pitchfork she was using to muck out Topsy's stall. "Okay, I admit it," she said to Stevie, who had just pushed a large wheelbarrow through the stall's open door. "Maybe Lisa's job really isn't more exciting than mine." At that moment, she saw Jeremiah walk past the stall, followed by the reporter from *Star Struck* magazine. "Well, not much more, anyway," she amended with a grin.

Stevie pretended to fan her brow. "Is it hot in here, or is it just him?" she joked in a low voice.

Carole didn't answer. She had just felt something, the slightest trembling movement beneath her feet. Another tremor? "D-Did you . . ." she began. Then she let her voice trail off, feeling like an idiot as a horse and rider trotted past on the path in front of the shed row. A moment after the horse—an enormous bay warmblood— had disappeared from sight, the trembling stopped. She sighed. "Okay, it's official. I'm totally insane."

"It looks good on you." Stevie grabbed a shovel and started to fill the wheelbarrow with soiled straw.

"Thanks." The two girls worked in companionable silence for a moment before Carole spoke again. "This is fun, isn't it?"

Stevie paused in midscoop just long enough to shoot her a look of disbelief. "This?"

Carole giggled. "You know what I mean. This trip. Hanging out with Lisa again. Seeing fabulous Southern California."

"I guess it has been pretty cool," Stevie admitted. "But just for a visit. I could never, ever, in a million years live out here."

"Even if Jeremiah asked you to?" Carole teased. Then, seeing the serious expression on Stevie's face, she leaned on her pitchfork again and gave her a searching look. "What is it?"

Stevie gnawed on her lower lip for a second without answering. Then she shrugged. "Haven't you wondered?" she said. "Haven't you seen how crazy Lisa is about Lily, how much she likes working on this TV show, how she's always talking about the great weather and the beach and the interesting people? And her dad's here, and she gets along great with Evelyn—"

"Hold it." Carole stood up straight. "You're

not saying what I think you're saying, are you? Because if you are, you're crazy. Lisa would never want to live in California full-time."

"Are you sure about that? Because she seems to fit in here awfully well."

Carole was already shaking her head. Her mind flashed back to her phone conversation with Lisa, but she shrugged off the thought. It was too ridiculous to think about. She couldn't believe Stevie could ever consider it seriously, even for a second. "Lisa's home is in Willow Creek," she insisted. "That's where her mother is. All her friends. Alex. Prancer. Max and Deborah and the kids. *Us.*"

Stevie looked stubborn. "Fine. You're probably right. I hope you're right. I also hope we get Lisa out of here before all this Hollywood glamour you keep talking about sucks her in for good and she forgets all about us and Alex and everything else in her real life."

Carole shook her head. This was a bit melodramatic, even for Stevie. Still, she decided to let it slide. Stevie had had a tough few months. If she was feeling a little melodramatic, well, that was fine, just as long as it finally took her mind off the accident.

Trying to lighten the mood, Carole reached over and knocked twice on the wooden wall of the stall. "I hope we get her out, too. Actually, I just have one major hope right about now. That's that *all* of us, Lisa included, get out of here before the Big One hits." She grinned so that Stevie would see she was kidding—even if she wasn't, not entirely. Then she leaned her pitchfork against the wall and surveyed the stall. "Looks like we're about done. If you'll take that load out to the pit, I'll finish up here. Then I'm supposed to groom Conejo for his big scene later."

"Okay." Stevie picked up the handles of the wheelbarrow and pushed it out of the stall as Carole went to retrieve Topsy from his cross-ties in the aisle.

Stevie was smiling, still thinking about Carole's new earthquake phobia as she headed down the shed row toward the manure pit hidden in a small grove of scrubby trees beyond the last building. Carole was always so together around Pine Hollow that it was sometimes easy to forget that she had weird fears and failings and worries and habits just like anyone else.

Me, for instance, Stevie reminded herself, her smile fading as she reached the deserted manure pit. She sighed as she upended the wheelbarrow. *My problems may be miles away right now, but sometimes it doesn't feel like it.*

She had been making a real effort during this visit not to refer to the accident unless one of the others brought it up. Did they have any idea that it was still so much on her mind? True, she had managed to distract herself quite a bit, between enjoying the new sights and sounds and people in California and worrying that Lisa might end up staying here forever. But that didn't mean she had entirely forgotten the reason she was here. This trip was supposed to help her forget about all that stuff back home, but that might be part of the problem. Deep in her heart, Stevie had the uncomfortable feeling that by coming here, she was trying to run away from her problems. And she had never been the kind of person to run away from anything.

Still, she had to admit that it was a relief to get some distance from it all—from Scott's accusing stares, the reporters' pesky questions, even her own family's sympathy and understanding. Here at least she could relax and *act* normal again, even if she still didn't *feel* entirely normal. And maybe if she acted it long enough she'd actually start to believe it.

All this talk about acting is making me think I should be the one to stay in Hollywood forever, not Lisa, Stevie joked to herself. For a split second, she felt as if that wouldn't be such a bad thing. Then she caught herself. What was she thinking? She had meant what she'd said to Carole before. This was a nice place for a brief vacation, but no way could it ever be a permanent home. Not for her, and not for Lisa, either.

I just hope Lisa feels the same way about that, Stevie thought. She started to push the wheelbarrow back in the direction of the stable buildings. *Maybe it's time to find out for sure. Maybe Carole and I should feel her out on the subject later when we get some time alone with her. Just in case.*

"It's okay, boy," Carole crooned to the nervous horse. "You'll like this. I promise."

She held up the hoof pick she was holding. Conejo rolled his eyes at her nervously, backed away a step, then carefully stretched his neck forward to give the hoof pick a cautious sniff. He let out a snort.

"Come on, now. Don't be shy." Carole slowly moved the hand holding the hoof pick behind her back, then held her other hand in front of the gelding, palm up. "Give me a sniff so we can be friends. Then we can put you in some nice cross-ties and I'll pick all the gunk out of your feet. How about that, hmmm?"

The horse still looked uncertain. Carole waited patiently, spending the time admiring the gelding's glossy coat, his tousled but silky black mane, and the high, aristocratic crest of his perfectly proportioned neck. Now she understood perfectly what Matthew Reeves had told them

122

earlier about Conejo's personality. Standing here, it was clear to Carole that the big black gelding really was almost as timid as a bunny. But she could see that from a distance—or on a television screen—the horse's tossing head, rolling eyes, and constantly shifting feet could make him look fiery enough even for a villain like Nick Torrence.

Nick Torrence. Matthew Reeves. How much did character and actor really have in common? Watching the run-through today, Carole had been certain that the only way the actor could be so convincing was if he had a big helping of pure nastiness in his own personality. But now that she thought more about it, she wondered if that was necessarily true. For one thing, Matthew had seemed pretty nice when he was chatting with them before the rehearsal started. For another thing, Carole had seen enough of Skye's movies and shows to know that he could act a part that was completely different from his own personality.

"There's one more thing," she said out loud, keeping her voice calm and soothing. Conejo's ears pricked forward suspiciously. "I saw the way you acted with him, big boy."

The horse seemed a bit quieter when she was speaking, so she kept on musing aloud.

"Animals are good judges of character," she

said softly. "And you calmed right down and seemed less nervous when Matthew came over to us. You really seem to trust him. So how bad could he be?"

Carole didn't know the answer to that. Maybe animals had different ways of judging people than people did of judging each other. Maybe it was possible for someone to be a total lying, scheming jerk around two-legged creatures but still love the four-legged variety.

"Well, you know what they say," she murmured. "Better safe than sorry, right?" It wasn't as if it mattered that much one way or the other. Matthew Reeves was awfully cute, but he was hardly the only heartthrob around the place. Carole smiled as she thought of Jeremiah. Now *that* was someone she could drool over with no worries.

With a quick glance at her watch, Carole saw that she was running out of time. She had to hurry or Conejo wouldn't be ready in time for his scene.

"Okay, time to get serious, bud," she told the horse. "Let's get you into those cross-ties and get started." She took a slow, careful step toward the horse, still murmuring soothing words to him. He tossed his head and held his ground as she came one step closer.

That was when the ground lurched beneath her feet.

"Ah!" she cried involuntarily. This time there was no mistaking it. The earth shuddered and the water bucket hanging in the stall rattled against the wooden wall.

Conejo felt it, too. His eyes started to roll again, and he jumped to one side.

Time suddenly seemed to be passing very slowly. Carole gritted her teeth and reminded herself of where she was. No matter how scared she was, she couldn't let the horse sense it. She had to keep him calm so that he wouldn't panic and hurt himself—or her.

"Whoa, boy," she began, but she had to stop and swallow to keep herself from screaming again as the ground gave another violent shudder.

That was all Conejo could take. With a wild scream of fright, he reared up on his hind legs, his forelegs thrashing the air in front of him.

Startled and distracted by her own fear, Carole threw a hand up to protect her face and took a step backward. Her legs buckled as the ground heaved once more, and she let out a loud, panicky shriek as she lost her balance and started to fall sideways. As her head struck the wall of the stall, she thought she heard a male voice shouting to her. But she wasn't sure.

The next few seconds passed in a blur. Later, Carole wasn't sure whether she had actually passed out or if she was just so terrified that she couldn't think straight. Either way, she had a pleasant awakening. She was suddenly aware that she was being held in a strong, gentle grip. When she opened her eyes, which she had squeezed tight in terror, she found herself looking into the concerned brown eyes of . . .

"Jeremiah?" she croaked in disbelief.

"Are you all right?" The young actor continued to peer down into her face. "You hit your head."

Carole struggled to sit upright. "Conejo . . . ," she croaked.

"He's fine," Jeremiah assured her. "He calmed down as soon as the tremors stopped."

For the first time, Carole noticed that the ground had stopped shaking. "Then it's over?"

"All finished."

Carole gulped. She felt like a fool for panicking over another minor tremor. "I'm sorry," she said. "I mean, I'm so embarrassed. I'm not used to this kind of thing, and—"

"Forget about it," Jeremiah said gently, still cradling her back and shoulders in his strong arms. "I was the same way when I first moved to L.A. We didn't have quakes back home in Ohio."

"We don't have them in Virginia, either." Carole managed a smile. For the first time, she found herself wondering how she looked—and smelled. If only she had washed up after mucking out that stall. . . . She comforted herself with the fact that Jeremiah didn't seem to notice. In fact, his concerned face was moving closer to hers than ever.

"How does your head feel?" he asked. He lifted one hand and gently pushed back a few dark curls that had escaped from her braid. His fingers probed her forehead gently. "Does this hurt?"

"No." Carole could barely push the single word out of her throat. She could hardly breathe. Was this really happening? Or had Conejo kicked the sense out of her, and was this all some kind of feverish dream?

Then Jeremiah's finger found a sore spot, making her wince. "Oops, sorry," he said quickly. "Do you mind if I push your hair away and take a look?"

"Go ahead." Carole took a deep breath. It was true, then. The pain, though minor, had been real enough. "It doesn't feel very bad, though."

Jeremiah examined the spot, being careful not to touch it again. "I think you'll be okay," he reported. "No blood or anything. You'll probably just end up with a bruise." He let her hair fall back in place and smiled at her. "You won't even need to mess up that lovely face of yours with some big, ugly bandage."

Carole's head was spinning, and she was pretty sure her bump had nothing to do with it. She had no idea what to say.

Luckily, Jeremiah didn't seem to expect a response. His grip tightened slightly around her shoulders. Was he actually pulling her closer?

"You must have been pretty quick in there to keep out of Conejo's way," he murmured, gazing into her eyes. "But I shouldn't be surprised. I've noticed the way you've been handling the horses today, and you really know what you're doing. I've never seen someone with such a natural way with them. That's very special, you know, Carole."

He called me Carole, she thought gleefully. *He remembered my name. Jeremiah Jamison remembered my name!* It was such a small thing, but it made her feel good. It even made her feel more than ever that she had dropped into the middle of one of her own Hollywood fantasies.

But in a fantasy, I wouldn't be wearing these grubby jeans, Carole reminded herself. *And I'd smell like roses or something instead of manure and horse sweat.*

Then her thoughts ceased as Jeremiah fell silent and simply gazed at her for a long, strange, breathless, magical, unreal moment. Carole couldn't do anything but stare back, drinking in his intense brown eyes, now so close to hers. Her body was frozen in place, and her mind seemed to be frozen, too.

This time there was no question about it. Both of Jeremiah's arms were around her now, pulling her closer. His head moved slowly toward hers, as if the power of their shared gaze were drawing it toward her. His lips parted slightly, and Carole felt her own lips trembling as they waited to meet his—

"Carole!"

The sharp voice broke the spell of the moment. Jeremiah jerked his head back and frowned. Carole, gasping for breath, looked around to see who had interrupted.

"Skye!" she exclaimed, feeling herself blush. She scrambled to free herself, and Jeremiah let her go immediately. "What are you doing here?"

"Looks like I should be the one asking that." Skye folded his arms across his chest and looked from Carole to Jeremiah and back again.

Jeremiah had jumped to his feet. "Really?" he snapped. "Looks to me like you should be the one minding your own business." He glanced at Carole, then reached down to help her stand. "I'll see you later, okay? And that's a promise."

He gave her a quick squeeze on her upper arm, then turned and strode away.

Skye was still staring at Carole. "What was that all about?" he asked. "I mean, I'm sorry I interrupted. But I don't think you know—"

"Carole!" This time it was Stevie calling her name. "There you are. I've been looking all over for you."

Carole forced herself to smile. She didn't want Stevie or Skye to notice that her entire body was still trembling from the close encounter with Jeremiah, or that her heart was beating so fast it felt as though it might leap right out of her chest. "Did you want to make sure I survived the Big One?" she joked weakly.

"What? Oh, the tremor." Stevie shrugged. "Right. But actually, Summer and I could use your help. Fancy keeps coming up short on her rollbacks, and I remembered you had that same problem with Starlight last summer. Can you give us a hand?"

"Sure." Carole gave Skye one last glance as he shrugged and turned away, a puzzled frown on his handsome face. Then she turned to follow Stevie.

The fantasy was over—for now, at least. *I'll see you later,* Jeremiah's husky voice whispered again in her mind. *That's a promise!*

NINE

Half an hour later Carole was still in a daze from her encounter with Jeremiah. She had given Stevie a whispered overview of the highlights while they worked with Summer, but she was still dying to have a nice, long discussion with someone about the exact shade of Jeremiah's eyes and the precise way his arms had felt holding her. *So this is why other girls spend so much time talking about guys and romance and dating,* Carole told herself as she wandered down the stable aisle, looking for a way to be useful. *This is fun!*

She heard the approaching sound of clip-clopping hooves and turned to see who it was. She saw Lisa heading toward her, leading a fully tacked Conejo.

"Hi!" Carole called, walking forward to meet them. Suddenly she stopped short and gasped, remembering that she had left Conejo without a second thought after her moment with Jeremiah.

"Oh, no! I forgot all about his big scene. Did you—"

"It's okay," Lisa said quickly. "Skye told me what happened. He said you got distracted by the earthquake."

"But that's no excuse. I—"

Lisa interrupted again, this time with an understanding smile. "Don't worry about it. If your fear of earthquakes is anything like my weirdness about heights, I'm not surprised you forgot about Conejo." She winked. "Anyway, I'm the one getting paid here. I should be glad you and Stevie are willing to help out at all when you're supposed to be on vacation. You two could be sunning yourselves on the beach right now instead of hanging around here doing the same stable chores you've been doing all summer. So really, don't worry about it. It's no big deal."

"Oh." Carole cleared her throat. "Um, did Skye happen to mention anything else?" *Like that he caught me on the verge of making out with America's hottest teen TV star?* she added to herself, feeling her cheeks grow warm at the very thought.

Lisa shrugged. "What do you mean?"

So he hadn't told her. Carole should have known Skye wouldn't blab about catching her in a clinch with Jeremiah, even to Lisa. He was a

132

gentleman. Carole smiled and fell into step beside Lisa. "Well, let's just say the tremor wasn't the only thing that distracted me. You see, I was having a little trouble with Conejo, and then the tremor came . . ." She went on to tell Lisa the entire story, trying not to leave out a single juicy detail.

She was so caught up in her tale that she didn't notice until she finished that Lisa was frowning. "You mean you were going to let him kiss you?"

"What do *you* think?" Carole was surprised. Was she imagining things or did Lisa look disapproving? Okay, so maybe Lisa could be a tad bit conservative about certain things, but she was no prude. At least Carole hadn't thought so.

Lisa paused to let Conejo nibble at a patch of grass and gave Carole a serious look. "Listen, I meant to say something about this later when we had more privacy." She glanced around the nearly deserted stable area. "But it looks like I'd better say it now. Jeremiah is bad news. You're better off staying as far away from him as possible."

"What do you mean?" Lisa's words weren't registering. This was hardly the reaction Carole had been expecting to her exciting, romantic story.

Lisa frowned. "I mean, don't get suckered in

133

by his big brown eyes and all the rest of it. It's just an act. It's as fake as that goody-goody character he plays on the show."

Carole shook her head slowly. She had known Lisa for a long time, and she knew that she was sensible and cautious. Still, this was ridiculous. Didn't she *ever* just let herself go with the flow, do what felt good? Had she learned nothing from hanging out with Stevie all these years?

"Look, whatever." Carole tried to keep her tone light. She didn't want Lisa to know how irritating that know-it-all voice of hers was sounding just then. "It's no big deal, okay?"

"It is a big deal if you're thinking about spending any more time with him." Lisa glanced at her watch, then clucked to Conejo to get him moving again. After snatching one last mouthful of grass, the horse obeyed. "You have no idea what he's really like. Believe me, he has nothing in common with that nice, honest character he plays. He's older than you, too, you know."

Now Carole was starting to get really annoyed. How gullible did Lisa think she was? Just because she had never really had a serious boyfriend and spent more time at the stable than out on dates, that didn't mean she was a total idiot when it came to guys. Sometimes, she had to admit, her friends made her feel that way, even if they didn't mean to. After all, Stevie and Phil were practically an old married couple, and even before Alex came along Lisa had had guys falling all over her. . . .

"You don't have to worry," Carole said, doing her best to keep her voice even and neutral. "It's not like I'm madly in love with the guy or anything. I just said he was cute." That was true enough. Carole wasn't looking for true love here—she might not be as sensible as Lisa, but even she knew there was no real future in a relationship between herself and a gorgeous TV star. She knew that just because Jeremiah thought she was cute enough to kiss didn't mean he'd be showing up for her junior prom next year.

But so what? Carole thought. *I can still have some fun with him this week while I'm here. What harm could there be in a little smooching with a handsome TV star? Especially one who obviously finds me so irresistible!* She smiled a little at that thought. Carole knew that her friends thought she was attractive; they had told her so. But when she looked in the mirror, she still wasn't sure what to think of her own looks. *Still, if Jeremiah Jamison wants to tell me I'm lovely, who am I to argue?*

Lisa was peering anxiously at her over her shoulder as she continued to walk Conejo down the path leading to the main part of the set. "Look, Carole. I don't want to tell you what to do. But as your friend, I'm telling you exactly what I think. Jeremiah is bad news, and the next time you see him, you'd be better off running in the opposite direction. Otherwise you might get hurt."

Right, Carole thought sourly. *And I just might manage to have some fun, too. What a tragedy* that *would be.* "Message received," she told Lisa shortly. "Look, I'd better go see if Stevie needs any more help." She whirled and hurried off, heading back toward the stable row.

"Carole, wait!" Lisa called after her. "Come back."

Carole pretended not to hear her. She ducked down one of the shed rows, knowing that Lisa couldn't follow or try to find her until after she delivered Conejo to the set. Then she smiled grimly. She wasn't going to let cautious Lisa ruin her fun. This could be her only chance to have a fling with a TV star, and she wasn't going to miss it if she could help it.

No matter what her oh-so-worldly friend thought.

"She looks good out there, doesn't she?" a familiar voice said from behind Stevie.

"Hey, Skye." Stevie turned from her perch on the fence of the largest practice ring. "How's it going? Shouldn't you be off saving the ranch or something?"

Skye grinned. "I don't get to do that until later. They're shooting some stuff with the guest stars right now." He hoisted himself onto the fence beside her and turned his attention to Summer, who was at the far end of the ring putting Fancy through a complicated routine.

Stevie followed his gaze. "She really is good," she said, admiring Summer's flawless seat and the precise, practiced way she handled the reins. "I have to admit, I'm a little surprised. The way she was talking this morning, it sounded like she'd barely spent five minutes in the saddle."

"That's Summer for you." Skye shook his head ruefully. "She's got more going for her than plenty of other actors in this town, but she just can't see that."

"What do you mean?"

"I mean she's talented—not just as a rider, but as an actor, too. She's smart. And you can see for yourself that she's beautiful." He shrugged. "But she's got one big problem. She's way too insecure."

Stevie wasn't totally surprised by Skye's comment. She had already spent enough time with Summer to recognize that the young actress lacked self-confidence. But just because she recognized it didn't mean she understood it. "I don't get it," she told Skye. "What does someone like her have to be insecure about?"

Skye sighed. "Who knows?" he said. "This is a tough business. You have to be able to take rejection and criticism, and most of us manage as best we can. But Summer takes it all to heart. She believes what other people say about her, especially if it's bad."

"Weird." Stevie was silent for a moment.

Skye wiped his brow with the back of his hand. "It's getting pretty hot out here, isn't it?" he commented.

Stevie smirked. "Is that a complaint?" she needled him. "I can't believe it. Everyone keeps telling me the climate out here is supposed to be perfect."

"Ha ha." Skye rolled his eyes. "Anyway, as I was about to say, it's kind of ironic that Summer landed the part of Caitlin Drake. Caitlin is supposed to be self-assured, manipulative, a daredevil—all the things Summer isn't."

"Too bad she's not a perfect match for her character like you are, huh?" Stevie teased, giving Skye a playful wink.

He chuckled. "Hey, what can I say? I *am* Devon Drake. But really, the casting people don't care that much what you're like in real life. They just want to know you can play the part you're supposed to play." He grimaced slightly.

"Obviously, this show proves that actors don't have to be anything at all like their characters."

Stevie was immediately interested. "Really?" she said. "What do you know? So good old Tinseltown really is the land of illusion. Who else besides Summer gets to play their opposite?"

"Well, there's Matt for starters. Matthew Reeves, I mean. He plays the biggest jerk on the show, but he's actually a really cool, easygoing guy with an amazing sense of humor." He cocked his head at Stevie. "Now that I think about it, you'd probably like him a lot if you got to know him."

Stevie was skeptical. "Hold on," she said, swinging her legs against the wooden fence post. "I saw that rehearsal earlier today. You're telling me that nasty guy actually has a heart of gold? And here I thought he was one of those cold-hearted, self-centered Hollywood monsters I've heard so much about. Next thing I know, you're going to tell me that scrumptious Jeremiah Jamison actually tortures small animals for fun."

Skye hesitated. "Well, not quite that bad, I guess."

Stevie laughed. "Yeah, right," she said disbelievingly. "What, then? He murdered his whole family? He sold secrets to enemy nations? He skipped the Academy Awards?"

"I don't like to talk about people behind their

backs," Skye said seriously. "There's too much of that in this business."

Stevie started whistling "There's No Business Like Show Business" until Skye gave her a dirty look.

"I'm trying to be serious here," he said. "But I feel a little weird about it. Look, did Carole by any chance tell you something? Um, something about her and Jeremiah?"

"How did you— Oh, right." Stevie gave Skye a knowing glance. "I heard you accidentally broke it up, huh? Too bad. Haven't you Hollywood guys ever heard of giving people their privacy?"

"Very funny." But Skye wasn't laughing. He glanced at Summer again. She was still at the far end of the ring, concentrating on her riding. "I didn't quite know how to say this to Carole at the time. But you're one of her best friends. I just think you should know that Jeremiah isn't the way he seems. He's not nice, and he's not sensitive. The only thing he really cares about is himself, and that means he definitely cannot be trusted."

"Really?" Stevie tried to reconcile what Skye was saying with what Carole had told her and with what she herself had seen of Jeremiah. It didn't make sense. She trusted Skye's judgment, but she couldn't help being skeptical. Maybe

Skye didn't know Jeremiah very well. Maybe Jeremiah got along better with girls than with other guys.

Skye seemed to sense her doubt. "Look, all I'm saying is keep your eyes open," he urged. "Carole's a great person, and I'd hate to see her get hurt."

"Me too," Stevie said immediately. "Thanks for the info, Skye." She decided it wouldn't be a bad idea to check out Jeremiah a little more closely, especially if Carole really intended to spend more time with him. Better safe than sorry.

"You're welcome." Skye smiled with relief. "Whew, I'm glad I got that off my chest. I mean, Lisa's been here all summer, so she knows how some actors can be, but I wasn't sure if you and Carole would see it." He waved at Summer, who was still putting Fancy through her paces. "In a way, people like Jeremiah are the exact opposite of Summer. She believes every bad thing she reads or hears or thinks about herself; he believes every good thing. With some people around here, worrying about yourself and your image can become an obsession."

"Wow. That's messed up." Stevie thought about that for a second. "It makes me glad I come from a place where I hang around normal people instead of a bunch of Hollywood freaks." Realizing what she had just said, she shot Skye a quick grin. "Present company excluded, of course."

"Of course." Skye was silent for a moment, and Stevie started to worry that he really had been insulted by what she had said. But when he finally spoke again, she realized he had gone back to thinking about Summer. "I'm glad Summer got to know Lisa while she's been here. Lisa's been really supportive, and I think she's been good for her." He glanced at Stevie. "Actually, she's been good for all of us."

"Right. Lisa Atwood, shrink to the stars," Stevie intoned dramatically. "And the stars' horses, of course. All your self-absorbed, frivolous actor buddies probably never knew what hit them. All they knew was their shallow, superficial world of make-believe was suddenly more . . . sensible."

Skye smiled at Stevie's teasing, though the expression seemed a bit strained. "When I told Lisa about this job, I wasn't sure she'd like it. Oh, I knew she'd love the horse part, of course. But I never guessed she'd fit in on the set so well and get along so brilliantly with all the difficult types here. She's really got a talent for dealing with people, you know."

"I know." Despite her jokes, Stevie was liking this conversation less and less. Not only was it becoming clear that Lisa and Skye were closer than they had ever been, but now Skye seemed to be saying that this whole Hollywood scene was practically Lisa's natural habitat.

Skye didn't notice her reaction. He was watching Summer again. "I don't know how we're going to get along without her," he went on. "She's made herself really valuable around here. I haven't really talked to her about it, but I think she'll miss us, too. I think she's had a better time with us this summer than she expected."

"Oh, really?" Stevie said, her voice sounding a little sharp in her own ears. "Are you sure about that? Maybe she's actually just *acting* like she's having such a great time—you know, like one of those actors you were talking about who fake whole personalities. Maybe she's actually just observing you all for the exposé she's going to write at the end of the summer. She'll probably call it something like *Lifestyles of the Overpaid and Undertalented: An Odyssey Through the True Hollywood.*"

Stevie realized too late that she had gone too far. Skye's forehead was creased with annoyance. "Okay, Stevie," he said, jumping down from his perch on the fence. "You can stop being so subtle, if that's what you're trying to do. It's clear what you think of Hollywood and show business and the rest of it." He shook his head as he brushed off his hands on his jeans. "I thought you knew better than to judge something without ever giving it a chance—you know, like way back when we first met, when you and your friends convinced me not to decide I hated riding before I knew what it was all about. But I guess I was wrong about you."

"Wait, Skye," Stevie began quickly. "I was just kidding around. But you don't understand—"

"See you later, Stevie." Skye was already walking away.

Stevie slumped down on the fence rail and watched his departing back. *He sounded pretty steamed,* she thought, feeling bad for a second. Then she shook her head. She might have gone overboard just a tad, but Skye had asked for it. Didn't he realize how hard it was for Lisa's friends to hear how great a time she was having? He'd made it sound like Lisa had been having such all-fired fabulous fun here this summer that she'd barely thought about her friends or her real home at all. Still, she knew he hadn't meant it that way. So maybe she shouldn't have made all those cracks about Hollywood.

But I couldn't help it, Stevie thought despondently. *He made it sound like Lisa loves it here so much she should never leave. That she might not* want *to leave.*

That was something Stevie didn't like to think about, and she was annoyed with Skye for putting the thought back in the forefront of her mind. How could he possibly understand how important Lisa was to all of them back home?

TEN

By midafternoon, the hustle and bustle around the stable had quieted a bit. Lisa and her friends were cleaning bridles in the spacious tack room. Lisa was still worried about Carole's interest in Jeremiah, but his name hadn't come up since their earlier conversation. She hoped that meant Carole had taken her warning to heart.

Aside from that one nagging concern, Lisa felt relaxed and happy. It was nice being with Carole and Stevie again. Really nice. She suspected they were starting to see why she liked California—and this job—so much. She hoped so. It would make it easier to readjust to returning home if they could understand and help her cope.

The girls were chatting lazily about the previous day's sightseeing when Rick poked his head into the room and took in the scene. "Still working them hard, Lisa?" he asked with a twinkle in his eye.

"It's okay. We're used to it." Stevie let out an exaggerated sigh of exhaustion.

Rick laughed. "I can tell. You girls are good workers. Almost as good as Lisa."

"Thanks, Rick." Lisa smiled at him. *Two compliments in a week,* she thought. *That must be some kind of record!*

She was so amused at the thought that she almost missed what Rick said next. "So why don't you knock off a little early today, Lisa? Show your friends around. We can manage here for the rest of the day."

Lisa opened her mouth to thank him again. It was a generous offer, especially after she'd taken off the day before. Still, she knew he was right. It had been a busy morning, but the afternoon was shaping up to be relatively slow. They could get along without her.

"You heard the man, Lisa," Stevie said excitedly. "They can manage without us." She grinned. "Besides, if they need any help after we leave, some of these TV stars can just call in their agents or masseuses or manicurists to fill in!"

The words hit Lisa like a sledgehammer. What was that supposed to mean? She frowned, her calm, comfortable mood shattered. She'd thought their hard day of work had proved to her friends that her job was for real. But maybe not.

147

Carole fluttered her eyelashes dramatically. "Fabulous idea, dah-ling," she told Stevie in a hoity-toity voice. "Let's do lunch! Better yet, let's hit the beach."

Lisa felt her hands clench around the smooth leather of the bridle she was holding. Her job was no joke. What could she do to make her friends understand that?

"Sorry," she snapped, feeling stubborn. "I wouldn't feel right leaving now. There's still too much to do here. I've got to make sure Topsy is ready for those close-up shots later, and someone has to finish these bridles before tomorrow's run-through."

Rick looked surprised, but that was nothing compared to the stunned, disappointed expressions on the faces of her friends. For a moment Lisa regretted her hasty words. What was she getting so worked up about? Carole and Stevie knew her job was serious—that any job that involved caring for horses was serious. Anyway, they were her best friends. She should be enjoying their visit and making sure they enjoyed it, too. Anything else was petty and stupid.

She took a deep breath, preparing a quick laugh and an even quicker apology. But as she opened her mouth to begin, someone bounded into the tack room.

"Hey, is this a party?" Jeremiah Jamison said

when he saw them all sitting there. "Why wasn't I invited?"

Rick murmured a polite hello, then faded out of the room. Jeremiah didn't seem to notice. He was too busy staring at Carole with a greedy gleam in his eye that Lisa didn't like at all. She had seen that look before—though luckily never directed at her—and she knew it meant trouble.

"Hi, Jeremiah," Carole said, in a soft, fluttery, breathless voice that made Lisa feel queasy. "We were just talking about going sightseeing. But Lisa can't make it."

"Bummer." Jeremiah shot Lisa a quizzical glance.

She scowled at him, annoyed at his interruption. She could almost see the wheels in his head turning, figuring out how this situation might affect him and what he could do to twist it around to his advantage. It was irritating how casually handsome he looked as he turned to smile at Carole.

"Just because Lisa can't make it doesn't mean you should miss out, Carole," he said smoothly. "I don't have any more scenes today, so I'm free as a bird. How about it? Want to see the town with me instead?"

Carole's brown eyes widened. "Sure, Jeremiah. That would be great!"

Lisa opened her mouth to protest. Then she

snapped it shut again and started chewing on her lower lip. What could she say? She'd already insisted she couldn't go. And she suspected her humble apology wouldn't sound quite as sincere now that Jeremiah was in the picture.

Still, she couldn't just let Carole go off gallivanting around L.A. with Jeremiah. She didn't trust him as far as she could drop-kick him.

She cast an anxious glance at Stevie, wishing she'd had a chance to discuss this with her. Carole was clearly so smitten that she wasn't listening to reason, but maybe Lisa could have made Stevie understand that Jeremiah was a total sleazeball, despite what his publicist and *Star Struck* magazine would have the world believe. She had already seen the way he'd treated previous romantic interests. He loved the thrill of the chase, but once he'd won someone over the same thing always happened. It might take a day, it might take a week, but he ended up treating her like dirt. She couldn't bear the thought of his putting Carole through that sort of heartbreak.

Stevie didn't return her glance. She was staring thoughtfully at Jeremiah.

"That's so nice of you, Jeremiah," Stevie said cheerfully. "I think I'll come along, too. It should be fun."

Jeremiah shot Stevie an irritated look. It was clear that what he'd had in mind was a one-on-

one experience. But he nodded grudgingly. "Sure, uh, Stevie," he muttered. "It'll be a blast."

Lisa let out a small sigh of relief. She still didn't like the idea of Carole being with Jeremiah. But at least now they wouldn't be alone. "I guess it's all settled then," she said, trying not to sound as depressed as she felt. What else could she say at this point? "We can all meet up again back at Dad's house this evening, okay?"

A moment later her friends and Jeremiah had gone. Lisa sank down on a stool and buried her head in her hands. What was wrong with her, anyway? She had single-handedly managed to ruin her own day because of simple stubborn pride. And along the way, she had made this whole mess with Carole and Jeremiah even worse by practically sending them an engraved invitation to go off together. What was she trying to prove?

"Lisa?" A familiar voice spoke uncertainly from the doorway. "Are you all right?"

Lisa looked up and saw Skye standing there staring at her. "Hi, Skye," she said, forcing a feeble smile. "I'm okay. Just mad at myself, that's all."

"Want to talk about it?" Skye stepped into the room and grabbed a bucket. Overturning it in front of Lisa, he perched on it and waited.

Lisa hesitated. But it didn't take her long to

decide that she would feel better if she got this off her chest, especially to an understanding friend like Skye.

He listened quietly as she told him the whole story. Then he leaned back slightly on his makeshift stool, looking thoughtful.

"First of all, I don't blame you for being worried about Carole," he said. "She's a smart girl, but Jeremiah makes a hobby out of making fools of all sorts of girls, smart or not."

"I know. And Carole really isn't that experienced with guys. . . ." She clenched her fists in her lap. "I wish I hadn't been such an idiot! Then she wouldn't have gone off with him."

Skye nodded sympathetically. "Don't beat yourself up about it. What's done is done. And I'm sure it'll be okay. What can happen, really? Especially with Stevie along."

"Knowing Jeremiah, he'll ditch her as soon as he can."

"Knowing Stevie, he won't be able to," Skye countered. "I had a talk with her a little while ago." He hesitated. "You know I don't like to tell other people's secrets, but I thought maybe she could help save Carole from some heartbreak if she knew the real deal."

"So she knows Jeremiah's a jerk?" Lisa could hardly believe it. A feeling of relief washed over her. If Stevie even suspected that there might be trouble in Carole's personal Hollywood paradise, there was no way Jeremiah would be able to shake her. She could be tougher than a bulldog when she was protecting her friends.

Skye wasn't finished. "As for the rest of it, I can't say I understand exactly why you didn't want to go, but—"

"It wasn't that I didn't want to," Lisa broke in. "I did. But I didn't want them to think my job is just some cushy little hobby that I can blow off whenever I want to."

"Do you really think they feel that way?"

Lisa sighed. "Well, no. I know they probably don't." She thought back over exactly what her friends had said. "Okay, I'm sure they don't. They were just kidding around. I guess I'm just a little sensitive right now because everything seems so disjointed."

"You mean because the summer's almost over?" he asked softly.

Lisa nodded, staring thoughtfully at her hands in her lap. "I thought I'd be dying to get home by now. And I am, sort of. But some conflicted part of me actually wants to . . . well, to stay. Do you think that's weird?"

"I'm probably the wrong person to ask about that." Skye scooted his bucket a few inches

153

closer. "Because I want you to stay, too. And I'm not conflicted about it at all."

"Thanks," Lisa said, still looking down. "But seriously, what should I do?"

"Seriously," Skye replied, "I'm too biased to give you any useful advice." Something in his voice made Lisa look up. He was looking at her steadily, and his expression was very serious. "If it were up to me, you'd never leave."

"Oh," Lisa said in a small voice. She wasn't sure what else to say. She wasn't even sure what was happening, except that she knew that her heart had suddenly starting beating double-time.

"When we first met you were, what, twelve? thirteen?" Skye smiled at the memory. "Definitely too young for a cool teenager like I was then to even consider as, well, you know. No matter how cute you were. Somehow, though, a few years' difference in our ages just doesn't seem that important anymore. You know?"

"I guess so," Lisa said softly, her head spinning. This was too weird! She and Skye were friends. They had always been friends. Even if she, too, had harbored a few thoughts about . . . well, anyway, that was all in the past now. "I have a boyfriend, Skye. And I love him a lot."

"I know." Skye nodded quickly, still looking

at her intently. "You and Alex are serious about each other, and I respect that. I'm glad you found someone to care about. And I definitely don't want to make things awkward between us. I hope we'll always be friends, Lisa. I'm counting on it. All I'm trying to say here is that I've been thinking a lot lately about what might have been." He paused and looked away, avoiding her eyes. "And what could maybe be right now if things were different."

"Oh," Lisa said again, flustered. She couldn't believe they were having this conversation. It was flattering but terribly confusing at the same time. Because if she wanted to be honest with herself, she had to admit that she had always noticed a special attraction between herself and Skye, something more than the simple, caring friendship the actor had with Carole and Stevie.

But what did that matter now? She was in love with Alex. She knew that as surely as she knew her heart was still beating.

"Anyway, I hope I haven't freaked you out too much." Skye stood up and gave Lisa a slightly sheepish smile. "I didn't mean to. But we've always been honest with each other, so I just thought you should know how things stand. I guess I could have played it safe and left it unsaid, but sometimes playing it safe just isn't the right thing to do. That doesn't mean I expect

155

anything to change between us, though. I know that's not going to happen. I just wanted to get it out in the open."

"I understand." She did, too—at least from Skye's point of view. He really hadn't told her anything she didn't already know or at least suspect. And she did respect him for taking the risk of being honest. A lot of guys wouldn't have had the guts to reveal their feelings that way.

Her own point of view was more complicated, however. As she said goodbye and watched Skye walk out of the tack room, Lisa's head was still spinning. She loved Alex. She loved her mother. She loved her home in Willow Creek. But things just didn't seem to be as simple as all that. Everywhere she turned these days she seemed to encounter tempting choices, new and interesting people, other ways of living that she hadn't known existed two months before. In a way, it would be easier if she'd never found out about them. But she couldn't quite bring herself to wish for that. Yes, maybe she could have spent a week or two with her father and then returned home to her nice, comfortable life in Willow Creek. That would have been playing it safe, as Skye might say. But she knew it wouldn't have been the right thing to do. She would have missed out on so much. . . .

She sighed and grabbed a dirty throatlatch from the rack beside her, hoping to distract herself with work.

Why did her life have to be full of such difficult choices?

ELEVEN

"Stevie, if you're having trouble keeping up, we could just meet you later," Jeremiah suggested casually.

Stevie shot him a dirty look. "I wouldn't be having trouble if you didn't rush off every time I stopped to look in a window."

Carole giggled. "Hey, Stevie, since when are you so into shopping?"

Stevie didn't answer. She was hot, tired, and annoyed. Here she was on L.A.'s famous shopping strip, Rodeo Drive—which didn't impress her all that much—and she was having all she could do to keep Jeremiah and Carole in sight. Jeremiah was clearly determined to ditch her if he could, and Carole seemed totally oblivious to it. Stevie suspected that her friend was so intent on making this a romantic, glamorous afternoon to remember that she'd put her brain on hold and was just going with the flow. That was the only explanation. Otherwise she'd surely see the nasty looks Jeremiah kept giving Stevie and hear the snide little comments he made whenever he thought Carole wasn't listening.

Jeremiah was on the move again. He had just grabbed Carole by the elbow and propelled her into a clothing store. Stevie rolled her eyes and followed as quickly as she could, pausing just long enough to let an elderly woman pass in front of her. She couldn't afford to be slow. She wouldn't put it past Jeremiah to duck into a dressing room or out the back door to get away from her. Unfortunately, she wouldn't put it past Carole to follow cluelessly without even noticing whether Stevie was still with them.

Stevie knew Carole had been working hard all summer. Taking care of horses was what she loved to do more than anything in the world, but even Carole couldn't really call it glamorous or romantic. So Stevie was willing to cut her some slack if she wanted to kick back for a while and have fun flirting with a good-looking TV star. Still, after what Skye had told her, Stevie didn't want things to go too far. That was why she had invited herself along, and why she had been gritting her teeth and putting up with Jeremiah's obnoxious behavior so far.

Stevie glanced around the clothing store, searching for Carole's familiar dark curls. The store wasn't very large or crowded, but there was no sign of Carole or Jeremiah.

Stevie frowned. There was only one door that she could see, and she knew they hadn't gone past her to go out. So where were they?

"Dressing rooms," she murmured, spotting a sign pointing down a hallway in the back. She hurried over, but all the stalls in the small changing area at the end of the short hall were empty. Where could they have gone?

Stevie returned to the main part of the store. It was empty except for the sales clerks. She bit her lip. Now what should she do?

She hurried to the door and looked out. Crowds strolled past on the sidewalk. The afternoon sun beat down on the scene. There was no sign of Carole.

"I really don't need this right now," Stevie muttered irritably. She stuck her hand in her jeans pocket, fingering the scrap of paper with Lisa's father's address and phone number. She could call Evelyn and ask her to come pick her up. Or she could call Lisa on the lot—no matter how busy she was cleaning bridles or whatever, she would surely come to Stevie's rescue.

Stevie sighed. No matter how tempting the thought, she couldn't abandon Carole. She wasn't acting very sensible right now, and she didn't have much experience with guys. She didn't know how rotten some of them could be, and she was obviously so blinded by Jeremiah's good looks that she couldn't see what a jerk he was.

She glanced down the street in one direction, then the other. This was going to be like finding a couple of lovestruck needles in a haystack. Still, she had to start somewhere.

I'll try going back the way we came, she decided. *If Jeremiah's half as sneaky as I think he is, he'll go that way just because he'll think I won't expect it.* She smiled grimly as she set off. *And if that's the case he'll find out pretty soon I'm not as easy to dupe as poor Carole is!*

She hurried down the block, scanning the crowds for familiar faces. As she walked, she also glanced into each store.

Despite her careful searching, she almost missed them. She was walking right past a bench on the sidewalk when she noticed them sitting there. They didn't notice her at all. That was because they were too wrapped up in each other. They were kissing passionately, their eyes closed and their arms holding each other tight.

At Stevie's loud gasp of surprise, Carole started and looked up, pulling back from Jeremiah's embrace. "Stevie!" she cried.

Jeremiah looked up, too. "Stevie," he said flatly.

161

Stevie noticed that his hand was still caressing Carole's back. She felt stupid for interrupting so bluntly, especially since she could tell that Carole was annoyed. Still, she couldn't feel that guilty about it when she glanced at Jeremiah and saw the look of pure venom on his face. She shuddered. Whatever Carole thought about it, Stevie couldn't feel too bad about interrupting her makeout session with him. It was becoming painfully obvious—to Stevie, anyway—that Skye was right. TV star or not, Jeremiah Jamison was trouble. She was glad she and her friends would never have to see him again after this trip was over.

Well, except on TV, she added to herself ruefully.

"Um, hi," she said, feeling awkward. "I was looking for you guys."

"Obviously." Jeremiah's voice was full of scorn. He abruptly withdrew his arms from around Carole and stood up. Stevie just glared at him. She was tired of pretending she didn't know what he was all about.

Carole jumped to her feet, too. She looked flustered. "Sorry we got separated, Stevie," she said breathlessly, obviously trying to smooth things over. "We figured we'd wait here until you caught up. Right, Jeremiah?"

Jeremiah just shot Carole a cold glance.

"Whatever," he muttered. "See you around." He stalked away.

Carole's jaw dropped. "Wait!" she called uncertainly. "What about the tour? You promised to show us . . ." Her voice trailed off. He was already lost in the crowd. She turned to Stevie with a look of confusion on her face.

Stevie felt bad for her, but she couldn't help feeling relieved, too. "Don't worry about it. We'll have a better time without him."

"Do you think it was something I said?" Carole stared off again in the direction Jeremiah had gone. "I mean, he left so suddenly."

Stevie shrugged. The last thing she felt like doing was making excuses for Jeremiah, though she suspected that was what Carole wanted. "Who knows? But like I said, we're probably better off without him." *We'd all be a lot better off without any of these California people messing up our lives,* she added silently. *If only Lisa's parents had never gotten divorced. If only Lisa's dad had never moved out here.*

She sighed and averted her eyes from Carole's perplexed, hurt expression and completed the thought.

Most important of all, if only Lisa—and the rest of us—had stayed home in Willow Creek where we belong!

TWELVE

"I mean, it must have been some kind of misunderstanding," Carole mused later that evening. She was sitting with her friends on the small porch off the kitchen of the Atwoods' house, looking at the stars and digesting the delicious dinner they had all helped make.

"Sure, Carole," Stevie said lazily, leaning back more comfortably in her chair. "That was probably it."

Carole nodded. She had already convinced herself that Jeremiah's abrupt departure had all been a silly mistake. Secretly she suspected that Stevie was probably to blame for it somehow. Still, she wasn't going to hold a grudge about it. It had been clear that Stevie and Jeremiah weren't getting along, and Carole was pretty sure it was because Jeremiah hadn't wanted Stevie to come along on their tour. He had wanted Carole all to himself.

She closed her eyes and sighed happily, allowing herself to sink into another daydream about their kiss. She had only kissed a few other guys before this, but she was sure that Jeremiah had to be the best kisser in the world. His arms had been so strong but gentle as they pulled her close, and his eyes had looked so gentle as they drew her toward him. . . . It had been a magical moment that Carole wanted to savor fully so that she would never forget a single detail. She knew she was going to fall asleep that night already dreaming of Jeremiah.

Stevie cast Carole a worried glance. She had that dreamy look on her face again—the look that told the world she was thinking about Jeremiah. Stevie didn't much care for that look, but there didn't seem to be a lot she could do about it. She hadn't had the heart to burst Carole's bubble by telling her what Skye had said. Instead, she had held a brief, whispered conference with Lisa while Carole was in the shower before dinner. But Lisa had seemed almost as distracted as Carole herself and hadn't had much to contribute.

Well, we're only here for two more days, Stevie told herself. *I'll just have to do my best to keep an eye on Carole tomorrow.* The girls had already decided to go to work with Lisa again the next day.

Lisa was worried about Carole, too. But she was even more worried about herself. The strangest thoughts had been popping into her mind for the past few days, and especially since her talk with Skye. The strangest one of all was the one that told her that heading back to Willow Creek wasn't her only option. She didn't want to just slide along with the current, playing it safe and doing what everyone expected her to do. If she went back to Willow Creek, she wanted it to be her choice. And if she decided to talk to her father about staying with him and going to school in California in the fall . . . well, that was simply another option to consider.

She checked her watch. Nine o'clock.

What do you think I should do, Alex? she wondered, raising her eyes to the moon. She missed him so much. But she knew very well what his answer would be. Like Skye, he was too biased to give her any useful advice. So were her friends— that was why she hadn't said anything to them yet about her thoughts. But she knew she would have to bring it up soon. They had already asked a few times about the exact date of her return, and she hadn't given them an answer.

Lisa sighed. She was going to have to make her decision quickly. And she was going to have to do it on her own.

When the girls arrived on the set the next day, Carole immediately began looking for Jeremiah.

She wanted to thank him for the day before, maybe feel him out about getting together again that evening. Lisa had said something about going dancing at a teen club on the beach, and Carole couldn't imagine anything more romantic than dancing the night away with her very own teen heartthrob.

She didn't see him for the first couple of hours. Luckily she was kept so busy helping with the horses that the time passed quickly. Finally, as she was picking out the feet of a tall chestnut, she heard his voice coming from nearby.

"What is this, anyway, a self-service stable?" Jeremiah was saying rather peevishly. "I'm supposed to be starting my run-through in fifteen minutes."

Carole dropped the chestnut's hoof and poked her head out of the stall. She saw Jeremiah standing a few yards down the aisle with his hands on his hips, glaring at Lisa. His mouth was twisted into an angry scowl.

"It's okay, Jeremiah," Lisa said soothingly. "I was just going to get the tack. Jeeves will be ready in plenty of time."

"Jeremiah!" Carole called, quickly letting herself out of the stall and latching it behind her. She hurried down the aisle toward him, a big smile on her face.

The smile faded when she got a closer look at

his expression. It hadn't changed as he turned his attention from Lisa to her. "Oh, it's you," he said coldly.

Carole stopped short. This wasn't the greeting she had expected, not after yesterday. Not after his lips had explored her own so tenderly. Not after he had told her she was the prettiest and sweetest and most interesting girl he'd met in a long, long time.

"Um, hi," she went on uncertainly. "How are you today?"

Jeremiah didn't bother to respond. A tall, striking brunette, an actress who played one of the minor characters on the show, had just turned down the stable aisle. Jeremiah was staring at her intently, an appreciative smile playing around the corners of his mouth. "How's it going, Erica?" he called casually as she came a few steps closer.

The actress looked surprised for a second but quickly composed her face into a nonchalant smile. "Hey, Jeremiah. Could be worse, I guess."

A strange feeling was taking over Carole's mind, making her feel as though she were watching the scene from the middle of a dense smog that kept her from seeing things clearly. Was this really the same guy she had spent the afternoon with just yesterday? How could his attitude toward her have changed so dramatically from one day to the next? Had she done or said something awful without realizing it?

"Jeremiah?" she said hesitantly, glancing nervously from Jeremiah to Erica to Lisa, her gaze finally settling on Jeremiah once again. She had to find out what was going on. That was all she could concentrate on. Something was terribly wrong, and she couldn't fix it until she knew what it was. "Um, do you think we could talk?"

"Carole, no!" Lisa's whisper was barely audible, though when Carole glanced at her, her face was stricken. But why? What was happening here?

Jeremiah finally tore his gaze away from Erica and turned to look at Carole once again. "Why would I waste my time talking to a kid like you?" His tone was still casual, almost lazy. But his gaze never wavered from her face. As she watched, almost mesmerized, he gave her an ice-cold smile that never reached his eyes. "By the way, could you thank your friend Stevie for me?"

"Stevie?" Carole felt numb and stupid as she struggled to keep up with this strange conversation. "Why?"

This time his eyes were downright cruel. He paused briefly, glancing at Erica and Lisa as if to be sure they were hearing every word. "For rescuing me yesterday, of course," he said. "As soon as we kissed, I knew it was a mistake. You were slobbering all over me like some kind of preteen who's been practicing on her pillow a little too much."

The words hit her like a rough slap. Carole felt her eyes well up with tears, though she fought to keep them from spilling over. From somewhere very far away, she heard Lisa gasp and Erica titter nervously. But the sounds didn't really register. She was too stunned.

Lisa was the first to react. "You—You jerk!" she said to Jeremiah through her teeth, taking a step forward with clenched fists. "How dare you talk to her like that!"

Jeremiah ignored her. He turned toward Erica, his nasty sneer replaced with a brilliant smile that seemed to show off every one of his even white teeth. "Sorry you had to see that," he said smoothly. "I just can't help losing my temper sometimes when these girls won't take no for an answer. Know what I mean?"

"Sure," Erica said automatically, returning his smile. She cast Carole one worried glance, but when Jeremiah gently took her by the elbow, she allowed him to steer her down the aisle.

Carole was still standing stock-still, her mind churning and heaving with what felt like a dozen earthquakes at once. Her mental numbness was wearing off quickly, to be replaced by a jumble of feelings—hurt, betrayal, confusion, and, most of all, humiliation. She had thought Jeremiah was a great guy. She had liked and trusted him. She had even kissed him. And now she knew that he had never really cared about her at all.

"Carole . . ." Lisa hurried to put a comforting arm around her shoulder.

Carole shrugged it off. "Leave me alone," she muttered. Even a best friend couldn't help her now. She just wanted to crawl into a hole and disappear. To be alone with her pain. "I've got to go," she murmured, turning to flee just as her tears spilled over at last. She barely heard Lisa calling after her as she rushed blindly away.

Through her tears, she noticed Summer Kirke letting herself out of Fancy's stall in the aisle ahead. The beautiful young actress spotted her at the same time.

"Hi, Carole." Summer spoke up hesitantly. She paused, seeming confused by Carole's tears. "I've been wanting to talk to you. There's something I think you should know. . . ."

Carole didn't even bother to respond. She just brushed past Summer and raced out of the stable.

Meanwhile Stevie was in a small paddock near the main part of the set, trying to convince Topsy to stand still long enough for a special-effects assistant to wrap his leg in fake barbed wire. It wasn't going well. The horse was balky and kept dancing away from the harmless plastic "wire," occasionally making motions as if he might kick. The assistant, who was young and obviously slightly fearful of the big animal, wasn't making much progress.

"Stop it!" Stevie told the horse firmly, gripping his halter. "This is no time to decide you want to give up acting."

"I've got to get this on him soon," the assistant, a thin, pale young woman, told Stevie anxiously. "They have to start shooting before the light changes. And Mel still needs to put on his makeup."

Stevie rolled her eyes. Horse makeup. This was exactly the kind of goofy California-type problem she didn't need. The more time she spent around this place, the less patience she had for the kinds of trickery and artifice that seemed to make up daily life here on the left coast. She glanced at the middle-aged, bearded man who was standing by with a palette of reddish body paint, ready to daub fake blood onto Topsy's leg to make his "accident" look authentic onscreen.

"Give me a break," Stevie muttered loudly. "You couldn't pay me enough to deal with this kind of idiotic thing on a regular basis."

Her impatience seemed to be catching. Topsy let out a snort and hopped to one side, shaking his head and stamping a forefoot. The special-effects assistant darted backward, out of range of his hooves. The makeup man cast Stevie a worried look. Stevie realized that her own foul mood wasn't doing anything to help the horse calm down, but she couldn't help herself.

She was so busy trying to keep her temper under control at the same time she was holding on to the horse that she didn't see Skye until he was right next to her. "Is that hoss of mine giving y'all some trouble?" he asked in a fake Texas twang.

Stevie shot him an irritated glance. "Spare me the stupid accents, okay?" she snapped. "Topsy's only doing what any sane horse would do by refusing to put up with this nonsense." She waved a hand at the fake barbed wire dangling from the assistant's hand.

Skye just nodded calmly. "Let's see what we can do, okay?" He glanced at the assistant, who seemed rather awed to be in his presence. "D'you mind if I give it a try? Topsy knows me pretty well. He may be calmer if I do it."

The young woman nodded mutely and handed over the fake wire.

"Hold him as steady as you can, okay, Stevie?"

"Your wish is my command," Stevie replied sarcastically. But she did her best to keep the horse as still as possible. Fortunately, Topsy had calmed down a little when Skye arrived. He turned his head to watch the actor curiously as Skye ran a hand down the gelding's side to his leg.

"Just tell me how you want it to go, okay?" Skye called over his shoulder.

The assistant managed to squeak out a few directions, still looking awed and nervous. Skye did everything she said, and moments later the fake wire was in place, looking quite convincing.

Skye smiled with satisfaction as he stood and gave Topsy a fond pat. "There you go. That wasn't so bad, was it, boy?"

The horse already seemed to have forgotten his nervousness. He ignored Skye's pat and stretched his head toward a nearby patch of weedy grass. The assistant shot Skye a grateful smile and scurried away as the makeup man moved forward and started working on the now distracted horse.

Stevie loosened the lead line to allow Topsy to graze. For some reason, having the ridiculous task completed made her feel more irritable than ever. It just reinforced her suspicions that nothing in California was straightforward and honest. It was all one big, bogus show, and she didn't like it. "Very impressive, Skye," she said sardonically. "It's nice to know if this acting thing doesn't work out you'll have a fine substitute career in faking horrible riding accidents."

Skye looked at her closely. "Is something wrong, Stevie?"

"What could possibly be wrong?" Stevie said, shrugging. "I thought nothing ever went wrong here in fabulous La-La Land." She tossed the lead line to him. "Here. You might as well take this. Your scene is starting any second." She stomped away without a backward glance. *Fake, it's all so fake,* she thought peevishly. Even Skye suddenly seemed to be just another part of it all.

She encountered Lisa halfway back to the stable. "Stevie!" Lisa cried, looking relieved. "There you are. Have you seen Carole lately?"

"I haven't seen anyone," Stevie replied sharply. "I've been too busy dealing with all your Hollywood buddies. Even the horses have egos around here."

Lisa didn't seem to be listening. "We've got to find her," she insisted. "She just ran into Jeremiah, and—"

Stevie cut her off sharply. "Then she definitely doesn't need us around right now. Three's a crowd—I definitely found that out yesterday." *And I'm not in the mood to be the extra wheel again anytime soon.*

"No, you don't understand. . . ." At that moment, there came the faint sound of a voice

175

urgently calling Lisa's name. "Uh-oh. That's Rick." Lisa bit her lip. "But listen, Stevie, you've got to—"

Once again, Stevie didn't let her finish. "You'd better go," she said flatly. She couldn't help remembering that Lisa was the reason they were all there. If Lisa had just put her foot down and refused to spend the entire summer in California, as Stevie herself would have done, everything would be different. For one thing, Stevie wouldn't have been driving home from the airport that fateful, rainy afternoon. She never would have gotten in that accident. Fez would still be alive, Callie would be as healthy as ever, Scott wouldn't hate her. . . . As soon as the thought entered her mind, a wave of guilt washed over her. She couldn't blame Lisa for the accident, she knew that. That was as stupid as blaming herself. Not wanting Lisa to notice how upset she was, she did her best to smile. "Sorry. I guess I'm a little on edge." Her apology sounded lame even to her.

But Lisa didn't seem to notice. "You've got to find Carole," she said urgently. "Jeremiah just dumped all over her, and she's really upset about it."

"Huh?" Stevie heard Rick calling Lisa's name again, but she ignored it. So did Lisa. "What happened?"

Lisa quickly filled her in on the scene between Carole and Jeremiah. "She ran off before I could stop her, and then of course I had to get Jeeves ready, and by the time I was finished—"

"Never mind." Stevie knew they didn't have much time. Rick's voice was getting more insistent. "Where is she now?"

"I don't know. She was heading out the end of the aisle toward that little patch of woods."

Stevie nodded briskly. "I'll find her," she assured Lisa.

Lisa shot her a grateful look. "I'll catch up to you as soon as I can, okay?" Without waiting for a reply, she raced off in the direction of Rick's voice.

Stevie headed in the opposite direction, her fury building slowly. *Who does Jeremiah Jamison think he is?* she thought heatedly. *He's even worse than the rest of these stuck-up Hollywood jerks. Just because he's on TV, he thinks he's better than anyone else. He thinks he can do anything he wants.*

She almost didn't see Matthew Reeves as she entered the stable aisle. He was leaning against the wall outside of Conejo's stall, looking relaxed and casually handsome in well-worn jeans and Western boots.

As soon as he spotted her, he gave her an amiable smile. "How's it going, Stevie?"

Even in the midst of her mood, made worse

than ever by Lisa's news about Jeremiah, a tiny, rational corner of Stevie's mind registered surprise that Matthew actually knew her name. She also couldn't help noticing that the good-looking young actor's voice was a rich, warm baritone and his bluish green eyes stood out even in the shadowy light of the overhang shading the stable aisle. But she wasn't about to turn into Carole, mooning over every pretty face. For all she knew, Matthew was just as big a jerk as Jeremiah, in spite of what Skye said.

Matthew still seemed to be waiting for an answer. "You want to know how it's going?" Stevie snapped. "Well, you'd better not ask unless you *really* want to know."

"Fair enough." Matthew's voice remained friendly despite her heated words. "I do really want to know, but only if you *really* feel like telling me."

Stevie wasn't sure what to say to that. And she didn't have the patience to figure it out just then. She had to find Carole. Letting out an inelegant snort, she hurried past Matthew without another word.

She didn't look back to see if he was watching her departure, but she imagined that those incredible eyes were boring into her back. She intentionally kept her pace steady until she reached the end of the aisle. Then she darted around the corner at full speed, almost running smack into Summer Kirke, who was coming around the other way.

"Oops!" Summer exclaimed, stepping aside just in time. "Sorry."

Stevie knew that the near collision was entirely her fault. But at the moment she didn't care. Everywhere she turned, someone seemed to be in her way. "Watch where you're going," she spit out angrily. "Or do TV stars always get the right-of-way around here?"

As soon as the words were out of her mouth, Stevie regretted them. Bad mood or no bad mood, hurry or no hurry, she had made a big mistake by snapping at Summer. The sensitive actress would probably go into a coma at her harsh words—or at least into a messy emotional outburst that Stevie would have to deal with. And she didn't have time for that right then.

"Sorry, Summer," she said quickly, making her voice as soothing as possible. "I didn't mean that. I'm just in a bad mood, and . . ."

Her voice trailed off as she realized that Summer wasn't really paying attention. The actress was glancing from side to side, looking worried and slightly upset but not as hysterical as Stevie had expected.

Summer finally turned her gaze on Stevie, seeming to realize for the first time that she had been speaking. "I'm sorry. I'm afraid I'm a little distracted. What was that?"

"Nothing," Stevie replied with relief. That had been a close one. "Um, I'd better get going—"

"Wait." Summer held up a hand and gave her a beseeching look. "I really need to talk to you. It's about your friend Carole."

Stevie frowned suspiciously. *What now?* she wondered. Her first impulse was to ignore Summer's mysterious comments and continue her search, but she didn't want to set off one of the actress's infamous anxiety attacks. Besides, she might have seen Carole. "What about her?" she asked cautiously.

Summer touched Stevie lightly on the arm. "Come in here where we can talk." She gestured to an empty stall. Stevie reluctantly followed, feeling trapped and impatient.

"Okay, what's the big secret?" she asked once they were safely inside.

Summer took a deep breath. "I didn't want to say anything before," she said. "I didn't think it was any of my business. But you should know that Jeremiah isn't the nice guy he pretends to be."

"That seems to be the consensus." Stevie thought back to what Skye had told her the day before, then to Jeremiah's obnoxious behavior toward her, then to what Lisa had just told her. She shrugged. "So he's a jerk. So what?"

Summer shook her head. When she spoke again, her voice sounded firmer. "He's more than a jerk. And I've noticed the way he and Carole have been looking at each other, so I—"

The last thing Stevie felt like doing was telling Summer that Carole's whirlwind romance was already over. "Carole hasn't quite been herself these past couple of days," she interrupted. "She's just trying to have some fun while we're here."

"Well, she's picked the wrong guy to have fun with." Summer bit her lip. "Jeremiah is a terrible person. I should know."

For the first time, Stevie felt a spark of interest in the conversation. Maybe Summer could actually tell her something useful—something that might help convince Carole that Jeremiah wasn't worth any tears or regrets. "Really?" she asked, keeping her voice neutral. She didn't want to scare Summer off. "What do you mean?"

Summer lowered her eyes. "Jeremiah and I worked on a miniseries together last year," she said, her voice so quiet that Stevie had to strain to hear it. "He pursued me from the first day we met. He acted like I was the only woman in the world. . . ." She paused and sighed. "Anyway, we ended up dating for a couple of months."

Stevie nodded. That part sounded familiar. "Yes?" she said encouragingly.

"Things didn't work out." Summer paused again, her eyes still downcast. "I tried to break it off with him. But Jeremiah didn't want things to end. He—He found something out somehow. A terrible, private secret that I didn't want anyone to know. He threatened to go to the press with it if I stopped seeing him."

Stevie was starting to feel queasy. This was even worse than she had expected. Summer was right—Jeremiah wasn't just another insensitive jerk. This went way beyond that.

"But that's blackmail," she protested. "Anyway, what kind of a nut would want to stay together with someone who didn't want to be with him?"

Summer shook her head. "He didn't care whether we were actually together or not," she explained. "He just wanted me to fake it in public. You know, for the publicity."

"Oh!" Suddenly understanding dawned. Summer had been an established star for several years and appeared often in movies as well as on TV. Jeremiah had obviously seen potential in linking his unknown name to her much more famous one.

"I trusted him." Summer's eyes were starting to look watery. "I trusted him, and he betrayed me in the most hurtful way he knew how. He can be so cruel. . . . He held that secret over me, and he still taunts me with it. I'm so afraid he'll want me to get back together with him now that we're working on this show together." She closed her eyes for a moment, regaining her composure. Then she opened them and looked at Stevie steadily. "Anyway, I just wanted to warn your friend so she doesn't make the same mistake I did. I haven't been able to speak to her alone, so I thought you could help."

Stevie gulped. *Some help I've been to Carole,* she thought guiltily. *I should have seen this coming.* She felt terrible. Summer's warning had arrived too late to save Carole from being hurt, and all Stevie could do about it was try to pick up the pieces.

"Wow," she said quietly. She glanced at Summer, uncertain whether to tell her what had happened or not. Finally she decided Summer deserved to know the truth. "Listen, can you keep a secret?" When Summer nodded, Stevie went on to tell the actress everything Lisa had told her.

By the time she had finished, Stevie was wondering if she had made a mistake by sharing the story. Summer's eyes were welling with tears again.

"He's clever," she said bitterly. "He knows exactly how to find a person's weak spot and use it against her."

The comment suddenly made Stevie wonder about something. "What does he have on you, anyway?" she blurted out before she realized what she was saying. "What could possibly be so terrible?"

As soon as she said it, a million possible answers flashed across her mind. She didn't know Summer. For all she knew, the actress might have murdered someone. She could be an alcoholic or a drug addict. Her father or aunt or cousin could be a spy or a mobster or an ivory poacher. Any way you looked at it, it was none of Stevie's business.

For a moment, she didn't think Summer was going to answer her nosy question. But after a lengthy pause, the actress met Stevie's eyes. "You trusted me, so I'll trust you," she said softly. "As soon as Jeremiah doesn't need me anymore he'll probably tell the world, anyway." She paused again. "I—I didn't always have this face."

"What do you mean?" Stevie felt confused. Images of science-fiction face-transplant surgeries popped into her mind.

Summer gulped, looking nervous. "I had surgery when I was a little younger than you are now." She gently touched her nose with the tip of one perfectly manicured finger. "It was my nose. I had it fixed."

Stevie nodded and waited for more, but Summer had stopped speaking again. "Then what happened?" Stevie asked at last.

"It was my fault, really." Summer shook her head as a tear squeezed its way out of the corner of one blue eye. "I should have destroyed all the pictures I had of my old nose. But I kept a few, and Jeremiah found them in my apartment one day. He still has one of them. That's the one he keeps saying he'll give to the press."

"That's it?" Stevie couldn't help being surprised. She could never imagine having plastic surgery herself, but she knew several people at school who'd had nose jobs. It wasn't that big a deal even in Willow Creek, let alone in Hollywood where Stevie assumed that sort of thing was practically taken for granted. "That's your horrible secret?"

Summer nodded, sniffling. "I don't know what I would do if he went through with his threats," she murmured. "It would be the end of my career!"

Stevie didn't think that was true. "Are you sure about that?" she asked, trying to be tactful.

"I mean, I doubt anyone would hold it against you even if they did find out."

"I don't know what I would do," Summer repeated, her eyes desperate. She grabbed Stevie's arm. "You won't tell anyone, will you?"

"Of course not," Stevie responded automatically. Her mind was already working. It was clear that Summer wasn't looking at this logically and that the situation was making her life miserable. "But listen to me for a second, Summer. Do you really think it would be so bad if people knew? Sometimes getting a secret out in the open makes it seem like less of a big deal. You might actually end up happier if this came out."

Summer's grip tightened. "You can't tell!" She was practically sobbing by now. "Please, I trusted you!"

Stevie was starting to see how Summer had gotten herself into this mess to begin with. She could also see that there was no way she would be able to convince Summer that having her secret out in the open wouldn't be the end of the world. "How about this, then?" she said, switching to another tack. "You could try blackmailing him back."

"What?" Summer looked confused.

Stevie shrugged. "You know—tell him if he gives away your secret you'll give away his. That he's actually a twisted, rotten jerk instead of the nice guy he plays on TV and in front of reporters."

Summer's eyes widened. "Oh, I could never do that," she protested faintly, looking horrified at the very idea. "What if no one believed me? I'd just look like a nasty person."

"But what else can you do?" Stevie was getting frustrated with Summer's passivity. "You can't let him get away with blackmailing you. Especially if you think he's about to start up again."

Summer shrugged and averted her eyes. "It's not so bad, really. It's just a few public appearances. And it's not as if I'm seeing anyone else right now. Anyway, he'll probably drop me again as soon as he manages to hook up with someone better."

Stevie didn't think she had ever heard such a string of lame rationalizations in her life. She hated the thought of a snake like Jeremiah preying on someone so vulnerable. Summer clearly needed help, and for a moment Stevie was tempted to step in and try to give it to her. *This is just the kind of thing The Saddle Club would have tackled back in the old days*, she thought, remembering the club that she, Lisa, and Carole had started soon after they'd met.

But thinking of Carole reminded her that she had other priorities right then. Besides, Summer was an adult. She was old enough to handle her own choices and her own life. Stevie had all she could do to deal with herself and her friends. After a few more soothing words, she excused herself and hurried off in search of Carole, leaving Summer alone with her problems.

THIRTEEN

"I still can't believe I was so stupid." Carole heaved a loud sigh and picked at the peeling paint on the arm of her Adirondack chair. "So much for my glamorous Hollywood fling!"

Stevie glanced over from her seat on the other side of the porch. The three girls had just finished a rather subdued dinner, and Mr. Atwood and Evelyn had shooed them out of the kitchen so that they could clean up. That meant the girls would finally have some privacy to complete the discussion they had begun on their way home from the set that day.

"Try not to take it personally," Lisa told Carole. "It could have happened to anyone. Jeremiah's broken more hearts this summer than you would believe."

Carole shot her a sour look. "That doesn't make me feel any better."

Stevie shifted restlessly in her chair. Carole had recovered from the state of total embarrassment and hysteria Stevie had found her in earlier, but she still looked upset. And somehow Stevie didn't think that sitting there rehashing the details of her brief relationship with Jeremiah was going to help cheer her up. It certainly wasn't doing much to improve Stevie's mood. "It's still early," she pointed out. "Why don't we go out and do something? Isn't there a movie premiere or an A-list party we can crash?"

Lisa looked thoughtful. "Not exactly," she said. "But some of the guys at work today were talking about going to Pacific Pulse tonight. That's this great teen club down at the beach." She smiled. "Skye invited me along my first week here, and I've been back a bunch of times. It's a blast."

Stevie did her best not to think too much about Lisa and Skye going out dancing together. She could worry about that later. Right then the important thing was taking Carole's mind off her misery. "Sounds like fun," she said, standing. "Let's do it."

Carole looked reluctant. "I'm not really in the mood for dancing," she protested. "I was going to go to bed early and put an end to this pathetic day."

Stevie grabbed her arm and dragged her to her feet. "Forget it. Jeremiah's not worth moping over. We're going to take you out and help you forget him!"

Soon the girls were upstairs in Lisa's room getting changed. Stevie's earlier enthusiasm had faded a bit, mostly because she still didn't like the idea that Lisa had her own room in this house. It made her feel testy.

She watched as Lisa pulled on a tank dress with a line of tiny beads around the neckline. "Hey, maybe this wasn't such a good idea," she commented. "When I packed for this trip, I didn't realize that spangles and sequins were part of the dress code. I don't have a thing to wear."

Lisa rolled her eyes. "I think what you've got there will be fine," she said dryly, nodding to Stevie's denim skirt and turquoise cotton T-shirt. "We'll bribe the bouncer if we have to."

"Look!" Lisa shouted above the noise of the pounding dance music. "There's Skye and Matthew and the guys!"

Carole turned and saw a small clutch of people from the TV show walking into the club. She sighed, trying to hide her expression from Lisa and Stevie. Now that more people they knew were there, her friends would probably want to stay even longer. Carole had been ready to leave as soon as they'd arrived. It wasn't that there was anything wrong with the club. If they had gone two days before, Carole would have had a great time. The music was good and loud, the people were interesting, even the snack food was tasty. Besides that, you couldn't beat the amazing view of the Pacific framed by the huge plate glass windows at the far end of the dance floor.

But tonight she couldn't relax and enjoy any of it. They hadn't been there five minutes before a guy had approached their table and asked her to dance. Carole didn't think her friends understood why she had turned him down, or why she had refused the next invitation, and the one after that. All she'd said was that she was in the mood to just hang out with them. But she saw the worried glances they exchanged with each other when they thought she wasn't looking.

Carole appreciated her friends' concern. But she didn't know how to explain to them how Jeremiah's rejection had made her feel. It wasn't that she had been in love with him—far from it. She hadn't loved him, but she had trusted him. That had been her mistake, and she was determined not to let it happen again.

Stevie had mixed feelings as Skye and the others threaded their way through the crowds of dancers toward the girls' table. Part of her dreaded seeing Lisa and Skye together in this setting. There was too much room for something to happen.

But the larger part of her was glad to see the guys. Maybe they could help her and Lisa deal with Carole, who was obviously feeling gun-shy after her encounter with Jeremiah. Stevie didn't like seeing Carole like that—not when she was already a bit of a late bloomer when it came to romance—and she hoped it didn't last long.

"What's up, ladies?" Skye called over the music as he pulled out a chair and sat down between Carole and Stevie. Matthew took the seat on Stevie's other side, and the other guys headed for the dance floor or wandered off to get something to drink.

"Not much," Lisa replied. "We were just waiting for some cool guys to show up so we'd have someone to dance with."

Stevie frowned. She knew that Lisa was just joking around with Skye and Matthew, but she still didn't like it. It sounded too much like real flirting for her taste. "Actually, we were just comparing California dance music to normal music," she broke in loudly, wanting to take both guys' eyes off her friend. "We decided California music has to be kind of weird to hide the fact that people out here can't dance to save their lives."

Skye turned to Matthew with a bemused smile. "Don't mind her," he joked. "That's what passes for humor out on the East Coast."

Matthew grinned, and Stevie stuck her tongue out at Skye. Before she could come up with a retort, she noticed a tall, skinny guy heading toward their table. He made a beeline for Lisa and shyly asked her to dance.

"Sure." Lisa smiled at him. "That'd be great. Thanks." She got up and gave her friends a little wave. "See ya."

Stevie found herself frowning again as she watched the pair find a sliver of free space on the floor and start dancing. "Does she know that guy?" she asked the table at large.

Skye shrugged. "I don't think so," he said. "I've never seen him before. Why?"

"No reason." Stevie fell silent, still keeping an eye on Lisa and her partner. What was she doing dancing with strange guys when she had a boyfriend waiting back home? Fortunately it was a fast song so there was no actual physical contact, but still . . .

Stevie was so busy worrying about Lisa that it took her a moment to notice that Skye was trying to convince Carole to dance with him. Carole looked reluctant, and Stevie's heart sank. If she wouldn't dance with Skye, a guy she'd known and trusted for years, she was even worse off than Stevie had feared.

But Skye wasn't giving up. "Come on, just one dance. Why should Lisa have all the fun?

Let's you and me get out there, Carole. We can show them how it's done."

Carole shook her head. "Thanks, Skye. But I'm not really in the mood for dancing. Why don't you and Stevie go ahead? I'll be okay here."

"No way," Skye replied. He leaned closer and continued in a loud stage whisper, "Stevie scares me. Her boyfriend Phil once told me that she's stepped on his feet so many times he had to have them amputated and replaced with bionic ones."

Stevie just rolled her eyes at the lame joke, but Carole giggled tentatively. "Well . . . ," she said. She still didn't feel much like dancing, but she felt bad saying no to Skye when it was obvious that he was trying his best to cheer her up.

"Come on," Skye wheedled with a winning smile. "I promise, the first time I step on your foot we can stop. Well, maybe not the first time. Let's make it the tenth time, okay?"

Carole couldn't help laughing at that. Skye was such a good guy—a real pal. And who knew? Maybe getting out there on the dance floor would improve her mood. It certainly couldn't hurt.

"Well, maybe just one song," she said.

Stevie smiled with relief as she watched Carole follow Skye out onto the dance floor. That was better. For a while there it had looked as if Carole was going to refuse to even look at anyone male. Maybe spending a little time with a guy she could trust, like Skye, would help remind her that most guys weren't as sneaky and rotten as Jeremiah.

Matthew shifted in his chair, and Stevie remembered she wasn't alone at the table. She suddenly felt awkward, remembering the weird encounter that afternoon at the stable. It didn't help that he was looking at her silently, a slight smile on his face.

"So," she said brightly, doing her best to hide her discomfort. "Do you guys come to this place a lot?"

"Once in a while," Matthew replied in his lazy, pleasant voice. "It's pretty cool, isn't it?"

Stevie shrugged. "If you like that sort of thing."

"Don't you like that sort of thing?"

"Maybe once in a while," Stevie allowed, her eyes skittering away from his direct gaze. "But I'm sure it would get tiring after a while. Kind of like L.A. in general, I guess."

Matthew leaned a little bit closer, looking curious and slightly bemused. "Don't you like L.A., Stevie? Why not?"

Because Lisa likes it too much. The answer sprang immediately to her mind. But of course she didn't say it out loud.

"Because it's so fake. So . . . so insincere," she said instead. "Everybody trying to be noticed, people trying to be someone or something else."

Matthew nodded amiably and was silent for a moment. Finally he spoke again. "That's not all there is to this place, you know. Otherwise normal guys like me wouldn't like it here so much. There's a lot to love about it."

Stevie grimaced. "Yeah, yeah, I know. The weather, the scenery and palm trees, *yadda yadda yadda*. I've heard it. And I'm not convinced. Give me four seasons and normal-looking trees any day."

She expected Matthew to argue, but he just leaned back in his seat. "Hmmm. Interesting perspective," he murmured. "So, do you want to dance?"

Stevie was startled by the sudden change of topic. "Uh, well, okay," she said. "I guess." She got up and followed him onto the dance floor, feeling decidedly strange. She knew her comments had been obnoxious, but Matthew hadn't seemed to notice. What was going on behind that relaxed, good-looking face of his, anyway?

The song that was playing had a strong beat, and Stevie was a good dancer. She noticed the appreciative look Matthew gave her as they started to move to the rhythm, and she couldn't help returning it. He was an awfully good dancer, too.

Though not as good as Phil, of course, Stevie thought loyally.

She gave Matthew a tentative smile, wondering if he was expecting her to say something. She didn't usually feel this tongue-tied around anyone, good-looking or otherwise. She wondered if her awkwardness had anything to do with those steady blue-green eyes of his.

She had to say something—anything—to fill the space between them. "So anyway, as I was saying back there, there's a lot to be said for cold weather. It makes you appreciate the summer when it comes, instead of just taking it for granted."

"I can dig that." Matthew smiled calmly. "I guess no place is perfect."

For some reason, his laid-back attitude made Stevie want to talk even more. "And that's not all," she went on. "There's just kind of a bad vibe here, you know? Like the people are all so self-centered they don't know how to have fun. Not like back home."

"What are the people like back home?"

Stevie shrugged. "I don't know, just normal, you know? They know how to be real people instead of big phonies. That's one reason why Carole and I couldn't believe Lisa was serious when she first told us she was coming out here to stay for the whole summer. We thought she was crazy. Especially since the three of us have spent almost all of every summer together since we were, like, twelve."

As soon as she said it, Stevie wondered why. She was just making conversation to be polite. So why had she told this virtual stranger something so personal?

Matthew was nodding as he continued to sway to the music. "That must be tough for all of you," he said. "But it'll work out. Things usually do."

"You never know. What if she decides she likes it better here? I mean, if all the ultraviolet rays have gone to her head or something? Where would that leave me and the rest of her friends back home?" Stevie paused. She still didn't understand why she was spilling her guts to Matthew like this. She barely knew him. But now that she'd started she couldn't seem to shut up. "Anyhow, she'd have to be nuts to want to live here full-time."

Matthew shrugged agreeably. "If you say so."

"I do say so," Stevie said tartly. "Frankly, I don't know how anyone can live here. On one hand you've got the earthquakes and the mudslides and all that stuff. Then, on top of that, you have to put up with all those smarmy, insincere Hollywood slimeballs. No offense." She glanced at him, but he didn't look insulted at all. Just interested. "Throw in a bunch of loser groupies, some smog, and about a zillion clueless tourists, and what do you have? A really lame place to live."

"That's one way of looking at it, I guess. But you've only been here a couple of days. How do you know you've seen it all?"

"I've seen enough," Stevie said flatly. "Believe me."

They danced without speaking for a minute or two. Finally Matthew spoke up. "You know, Stevie," he said thoughtfully, "you think too much about the past and the future. You'd probably be a lot happier if you just let yourself live in the moment once in a while." Before Stevie could figure out what that meant, Matthew took her firmly by the arm, just above the elbow. "Come on. I want to show you something." He steered her off the dance floor and toward a side door she hadn't noticed before.

Stevie was so startled that she didn't resist at first. Before she knew it, she was standing outside the club on a narrow sidewalk leading between two buildings toward the beach.

"Hey," she said indignantly, finally yanking her arm out of his grasp. "What's the big idea?"

Matthew let her go without a protest. "The

moon's up," he said. "Come with me if you want to see another side of Southern California." He turned to head toward the beach, tossing one final comment casually over his shoulder, almost as an afterthought. "Unless you'd rather just stick with your own opinion. That'd probably be easier, I guess."

After a brief struggle between annoyance and curiosity, Stevie shrugged and followed him. She couldn't resist a challenge like that. Anyway, it wasn't that late yet, and there were lots of people around. She would be safe enough—except from Matthew's strange and exasperating personality, of course.

She stopped short as she stepped out from the narrow path between the buildings and saw the beach spread out before her. The sky was dark except for a three-quarter moon that spilled its cool white light over everything, making the smooth sand and the whitecaps on the breaking waves appear to be the same silvery color. It was beautiful.

Matthew had stopped and was looking back at her, taking in her reaction. "Nice, isn't it?" he said casually.

She shot him an annoyed look. "Big deal. We have moonlight on the East Coast, too."

"I've heard that." Matthew's mouth twitched with amusement. "But if you'll humor me just a little longer, I think I can show you something you won't see back home."

Stevie sighed. She had come this far. What did she have to lose? "Whatever," she said, trying to match his own casual tone. She kicked off her shoes and carried them, enjoying the feel of the still-warm sand between her toes. "Are you going to tell me where we're going?"

"You'll see when we get there. It isn't far."

I should probably be nervous, Stevie told herself, lengthening her stride to keep up with Matthew's long, swinging step. *Haven't I seen a bunch of horror movies that start out this way?* But she couldn't make herself worry seriously. After all, there were tons of people strolling on the beach and even more thronging on the boardwalk just a few yards away. Besides, Stevie felt as though she had been worrying and brooding for a long time. When was the last time she had followed her nose to adventure? When was the last time she had done something new, something fun? *Probably about two months ago, I guess,* she thought ruefully.

So she kept quiet and followed Matthew down the beach, wondering where on earth they were going. If he thought she was going to be impressed by a little moonlit beach scenery, she had news for him. She'd already seen it. And she wasn't impressed. She still preferred the look of the moonlight filtering through the treetops during a late trail ride in the woods behind Pine Hollow.

They walked along in silence for about ten minutes. Finally, just ahead, Stevie noticed a rocky outcropping jutting out into the sand, stretching toward the breaking waves and hiding the beach beyond. Maybe that was where they were heading, Stevie thought. But why? Was it some kind of California lovers' lane? Was that what this was about? Somehow she didn't think so.

"What's that?" Stevie tilted her head and listened. The slight ocean breeze had just brought her a faint, familiar sound over the noise of the waves. "Music?"

Matthew grinned. "We're almost there." He broke into an easy lope, and Stevie jogged after him. The music grew louder with every step until Stevie recognized a recent rock hit. Was Matthew taking her to another dance club? But the music seemed to be coming from the beach, not the boardwalk.

Before she could figure it out, they had reached the outcropping. Matthew led the way over it, and from there Stevie could see a secluded cove just beyond.

Secluded, but not deserted. There were at least a dozen people there, some lounging on the sand near a cranking boom box, others in the ocean itself, surfing on the six-foot waves that were breaking rhythmically on the sand. There were guys and girls in a wide range of ages, from a sandy-haired kid who looked about ten to a pair of women who had to be older than Stevie's mother.

"Here we are," Matthew announced. He turned to face Stevie and gave her a long, slow, slightly challenging grin. "In the moment."

With that, he backed away and peeled off his shirt. He spun and raced toward the water, pausing just long enough to scoop up an unused surfboard lying near the boom box. As Stevie watched, he tossed the board over a breaking wave and crashed into the water after it.

Stevie hesitated. What was she supposed to do now?

Her first impulse was to go back to the club and find her friends. But she couldn't quite bring herself to leave the scene at the cove. There was something about the moonlight, the music, and yes, even Matthew himself . . .

"What the heck," she muttered. "You're only young once, right?"

She tossed her shoes aside, then hurried toward the boom box. "Anybody have a board I can borrow?" she asked the beach at large. One of the older women pointed to a neon pink board with aqua zigzags, and Stevie grinned. "Thanks!"

The board was heavier than she had expected, but she hoisted it gamely. As she ran toward the water, she glanced down at her skirt and T-shirt.

Good thing Mom only lets me buy stuff that's machine washable, she thought with glee. *Because here goes nothing!*

She raced headlong into the waves, shrieking involuntarily as the cool ocean water soaked her clothes. Matthew heard her and turned his head. He was paddling out on his board, stomach down.

"Come on!" he shouted. "I'll give you some pointers."

She nodded and concentrated on getting herself and her board out to where he was, beyond the breakers. She was a strong swimmer, so it didn't take long, especially after she got out far enough to emulate Matthew's stomach-down paddling. As soon as she was close enough, she slid down off her board. Treading water, she grabbed Matthew's board . . . and with a swift yank, tipped him off of it into the ocean.

Taken by surprise, he plunged under for a second and came up laughing, wet hair in his eyes.

"Hey!" he cried, flipping his head back so that his hair flew out of his eyes and stuck straight up in front. "Is that the kind of thing they teach you back East?" He swam over and, before Stevie could wiggle away, dunked her soundly two or three times.

That led to an enthusiastic splash fight. Finally Stevie's arms got so tired that she stopped and climbed onto her board again. "Truce?" she called over the roar of the waves.

"Truce," Matthew agreed. "Now are you ready for some *serious* fun?"

That was when Stevie's brief surfing lesson began. Matthew showed her how to pick her wave and demonstrated a few other basics in the relatively calm water out past the breakers. "Stay low and hold on, at least for the first few times. Don't try to stand until you get the hang of it or you'll fall off."

"Got it, Coach." Stevie nodded obediently. Then, when she spotted a wave she liked, she went for it—and once the wave grabbed her board, she stood precariously, her arms windmilling desperately as she fought for balance. She grinned as she heard Matthew's shout of amusement behind her. As she lost her balance for good and pitched off the board to one side, she saw him skim past expertly on his own board.

"Nice form—for a beginner," he called as she came up for air and swam to retrieve her board.

"Thanks," she called back. "I was just making a point. Stevie Lake is *not* afraid of falling off!"

After a few more tries, Stevie had the hang of it. As she swooped toward shore for about the tenth time, her clothes and hair soaking wet, her knees scraped from a wild wave that had caught her unaware, her eyes stinging from the salt water, she had to admit that she was having more fun than she'd had in longer than she could remember. She felt like a carefree little kid again, with all thoughts of car accidents, worrisome friends, and the uncertain future far from her mind.

For the first time in a long time, Stevie was living in the moment.

FOURTEEN

S tevie led a tall gray mare named Jewel to the mounting block at the end of the stable row. She swung aboard and settled herself in the saddle. "Ready to go?" she asked her friends.

Lisa nodded. She was mounted and waiting on Topsy. Carole had already ridden a few yards away on her horse for the day, a spirited bay, and was adjusting her stirrups.

Stevie waited until Lisa had swung Topsy around and headed toward the foothills at a walk. Then she followed on Jewel, enjoying the feel of the mare's long, smooth, easy stride and the warmth of the late-afternoon sunshine soaking through her thin cotton T-shirt. Carole quickly turned her horse to join them.

"It was really nice of Skye to arrange this for us," Carole commented.

Lisa nodded. "I guess he remembered how much we like trail rides. It was all his idea. He wanted you guys to have fun on your last day here." She cast a sidelong glance at Stevie. "Though maybe some of us have already had enough fun for one trip."

Stevie grimaced. "Ha, ha," she said heavily. Her friends had been teasing her all day about the previous night's impromptu surfing adventure, and it was getting kind of old. However, she had noticed that they didn't mention anything at all when Matthew was within hearing distance. She could tell they didn't quite understand where he fit into it all, and she couldn't really blame them. She didn't understand it very well herself.

She knew now that Matthew was nothing like the character he played on TV. That much was obvious. It was also obvious that she had felt an attraction to him that she had felt to few other guys. That didn't mean she cared any less about Phil, or that she wanted anything to happen between her and Matthew.

I wonder if that's how Lisa feels about Skye and Alex, she mused. *Maybe she's got some murky more-than-a-friend feelings for Skye. She can't help that if it's true, any more than I can help the thing with Matthew. But it doesn't mean she's going to betray Alex. It doesn't even mean she loves him any less. Does it?*

She wasn't sure. She could only speak for herself, and she knew that she was as committed to

Phil as ever. So maybe it was possible. In any case, whatever else she took away from this trip, Matthew's advice—to remember that life is lived in the moment, one day at a time—had struck a nerve with her, deeper than he would ever know. For the first time, she had realized that she wasn't just worrying too much over the future, she was also still stuck in the past. The accident had happened two months before, but Stevie hadn't moved past it in her mind. Callie had, Carole had, but she hadn't. She had been trying to blame other people for that—Scott Forester and his resentful looks, the TV reporter, even concerned friends who seemed to be constantly asking her how she was doing. By doing so, Stevie realized, she had been no better than Summer, allowing what other people said or thought to control her life. Stevie wasn't sure that Summer would ever realize that she had a choice about whether to give in to Jeremiah's threats. And there wasn't much that Stevie—or anyone else—could do about that. But Stevie finally saw her own situation a little more clearly, and she was determined to make a change for the better. It wouldn't be easy—Scott would still be there waiting to trip her up, and so would all the others—but all she could do was try. And take it one day at a time.

After all, Stevie reminded herself, *I don't really have any other choice, do I?*

At that moment Jewel stumbled over a rock, and Stevie snapped out of it. For a few minutes she had been so lost in thought that she had almost forgotten where she was. She glanced at her friends to see whether they had noticed how uncharacteristically quiet she was being. Even if she was starting to feel more comfortable with her weird feelings, she didn't want them to guess that she was still thinking about Matthew.

But neither of them was even looking at her. Lisa's face was pensive. Despite her new perspective, Stevie couldn't help wondering what she was thinking about, and her stomach clenched as she thought of her brother sitting at home, lonely and missing his girlfriend.

Then she shook her head. Those kinds of thoughts didn't help anyone. She might as well remember Matthew's advice, live in the moment, enjoy the trail ride, and try to forget about the future for a while. Because in this particular instance, the future would be up to Lisa. Of course, Carole had tried to live in the moment, and look where that had gotten her. . . . Stevie turned to check on her. Carole was staring straight ahead, her face sunk into the expression she had worn off and on for the past two days—pained, thoughtful, and slightly wary.

Carole didn't notice Stevie's glance. She was rehashing her brief involvement with Jeremiah for the umpteenth time. She still had trouble understanding how it had gone so wrong. How could he have deceived her so completely? How could she know instantly when a horse wasn't feeling well or was about to try something sneaky but not have the slightest idea when a person was out to hurt her? Was she really that clueless about guys?

She guessed maybe she was. She had always been more hesitant about dating and romance than Stevie and Lisa were. When they were all younger it hadn't seemed like such a big deal, but lately Carole had begun to feel that she was missing out on something, that she had been left behind somehow without realizing it was happening. Both of her friends had serious relationships, and that sometimes made it seem as though they were members of a secret club she wasn't yet qualified to join.

And right now she wasn't sure she even wanted to join. After what had happened, she suspected it would be a while before she was ready to trust a guy again, no matter how much he flattered her. Going with the flow had seemed like a good idea at the time, but now Carole knew that the price of a little recklessness and fun could be far too high.

Still, this trip hasn't been all bad news, Carole reminded herself. *At least I got to see Lisa again. And I think I'm finally starting to believe that every little tremor doesn't signal the start of the Big One.* She almost smiled at the thought. After surviving what Jeremiah had done to her, the idea of a little rumbling underfoot didn't seem so scary anymore. She still didn't understand how people could live in earthquake country, though. She would take the nice, still, solid ground back home any day.

Realizing that she had been quiet for a long time, she glanced at Stevie and Lisa to see if they had noticed. The last thing she wanted was for them to guess that she was thinking about Jeremiah and launch into one of their well-intentioned speeches. Luckily they both seemed wrapped up in their own thoughts. The three girls were so close that it sometimes seemed they could read one another's minds, but at the moment it made Carole a little uncomfortable to try to imagine what they were thinking. She had done her best to hide her shock that Stevie had gone off with Matthew, but it wasn't easy. The surprising part wasn't that Stevie had gone surfing fully clothed—that was just like her. But since when did she suddenly go from completely disliking a guy to blushing whenever she passed him in the stable? What did it mean? Carole wasn't sure she wanted to know. It just went to show that the relationships between guys and girls were more complicated than she had realized.

And then there was Lisa. Carole wanted to think that Lisa was so quiet because she was so overwhelmed with happiness at the thought of going home soon. But she knew it probably wasn't that simple. She had been so wrapped up with her quest for romance and excitement that she hadn't paid much attention to Stevie's worries at first. But now that it was almost time to leave, Carole realized Lisa hadn't said much about her return to Willow Creek. She hadn't even said that much about Alex. Did that mean Stevie's suspicions were correct? Had Lisa fallen in love with Skye this summer, or worse yet, with California? Was she actually wishing she could stay here instead of coming home?

Lisa was so wrapped up in her own thoughts that she wasn't aware that her friends were strangely silent as they rode. She was thinking back on all the things that had gone into making her summer in California so wonderful. It was hard to believe it was really coming to an end so soon.

Or is it? Lisa asked herself. *I don't have much time to make up my mind. I have to figure out where I belong—which place will be best for me.*

She knew that the easiest option would be to sit back and go with the flow. That would mean automatically and obediently heading back to Virginia the following week, just as everyone expected her to. But letting that happen would mean she wasn't in control of her own life. She was well aware that most people thought of her as a good girl, for better or for worse. Did she really have the strength to rebel for once, to make her own choice, even if that meant defying expectations?

She wasn't sure. She wasn't even sure what she wanted to do. She knew that her father and Evelyn would be thrilled to have her stay. So would Skye and her other friends on the set. Maybe she would even be able to work out a part-time job for the school year. Staying would mean she would get to watch Lily grow up, to be a real part of her sister's life. If she made that choice, her mother and her friends back home would just have to adjust. So would Alex, though Lisa was realistic enough to know that the prospects for continuing their relationship long-distance were iffy at best. Still, if they were meant to be together, they should be able to work it out. Right? It wasn't as if it would always be easy, anyway—Lisa would be leaving for college before long, and who knew what would happen then?

Though she was trying to keep her thoughts as rational as possible, Lisa's heart ached at the thought of being separated from Alex, being apart from Carole and Stevie. They had all been together so long. . . . Still, she had friends in California now, too. Maybe they weren't as close as her old friends yet, but who knew what could happen if she took the chance? Besides that, she had really loved working behind the scenes of *Paradise Ranch* this summer. Her job had given her the chance to see all the fascinating processes that went into producing a television show. She was even starting to think it was interesting enough to consider as a possible career someday. Of course, it was such a competitive business— the best way to have a shot at it would be to stay and get as much experience as she could.

Suddenly Lisa noticed that her friends were being awfully quiet. They had been riding for almost half an hour and nobody had said a word. She glanced at them and saw that they both looked thoughtful and rather somber. She guessed that Carole was still thinking about Jeremiah. And Stevie was probably back to brooding over the accident again, now that it was almost time for her to return home. Lisa didn't envy either of her friends their problems, and she knew she would do whatever she could to help them through. But she also knew that there wasn't much she could do in either case other than listen and be a supportive friend.

I just hope they'll be supportive of my decision, she thought. *No matter what it is. I know they'll try, even if . . .*

She sighed. This wasn't going to be easy. She was trying to sort the pros and cons of this decision into logical categories, but the borders of the categories kept melting and flowing into each other. If she stayed here, she would miss her boyfriend, her best friends, and her mother. If she went back to Willow Creek, she would miss her father and Lily and her new friends. Starting a new school in her senior year would be hard. But she would have opportunities here she wouldn't have back home. And so on, back and forth, seesawing in her mind. . . . In the end, she wasn't sure what the score added up to.

But that didn't mean she was giving up. She had made a promise to herself, a solemn promise to make this an active choice, not a passive one. A promise that she would do what she thought was best for her, not for anyone else.

And Lisa always kept her promises.

FIFTEEN

"Can you believe school starts tomorrow?" Carole commented, slinging Starlight's bridle over her shoulder and reaching for his saddle.

Stevie groaned. "Don't remind me," she said, already heading for the stable aisle with Belle's tack. "I'm depressed enough already. But I figure if I ignore it as long as possible, it will be sort of like jumping into cold water—the shock will stun me just long enough to get used to it."

Carole grinned. "Suit yourself. But I hope this doesn't mean you're backing out of our end-of-summer trail ride."

"Don't worry. Belle still hasn't forgiven me for leaving her alone last week when we were visiting Lisa. If she gets any friskier, she'll be ready to join the rodeo as a bucking bronco."

Carole followed Stevie out of the tack room. The two girls strolled side by side down the nearly deserted aisle toward Pine Hollow's

U-shaped row of stalls. All the schools in Willow Creek were opening the next day, so most of the younger riders were busy with parties or barbecues or last-minute shopping trips, and the girls had the place almost to themselves. It was always a bittersweet feeling to know that another summer was ending and a new routine about to begin, but this year the mood seemed stronger than ever.

Stevie decided not to think about that. "I'm glad Skye's show turned out to be so good," she commented. "You can already tell it's going to be a big hit."

Carole nodded. *Paradise Ranch* had finally debuted on TV the evening before, and a whole crowd of people had gathered at Stevie's house to watch it. Even Stevie's parents had agreed that the show was terrific—though Carole herself couldn't help feeling a pang every time Rand Hayden came onscreen.

"It was pretty cool to see Lisa's name in the credits, wasn't it?" Carole said, mostly to distract herself from thoughts of Jeremiah.

"Sure. And it's a good thing we taped it so we could rerun it in slow motion," Stevie joked. "Otherwise there's no way we would have spotted it stuck in there with all those other names."

Carole smiled slightly. "Don't worry. If she decides to follow through on her idea of a career in TV production, her name won't be lost in the crowd for long. You know Lisa never does anything halfway."

"I know." Stevie was silent for a moment. The girls reached their horses' stalls, which were next to each other, and let themselves in.

As soon as Stevie hoisted the saddle onto Belle's back, she noticed that the stitching on one of her stirrup leathers looked more frayed than she remembered. "Oops," she said. She finished tightening the girth, then detached the questionable leather from the stirrup bar and let herself back out into the aisle.

She poked her head over the half door of Starlight's stall. "I've got to go back to the tack room for a sec," she told Carole, holding up the leather. "I'll be right back."

She hurried down the aisle. Halfway there, she heard footsteps approaching from around the corner just ahead. A moment later Scott Forester walked into view.

He spotted her immediately. Just as immediately, his face froze into its now customary cold stare. He averted his eyes as they approached each other in the narrow hallway, as if it pained him even to look at her.

Stevie started to cringe and scurry past, as she had done all summer. But then she reminded herself of her new attitude. *I may not be able to control Scott's behavior or his feelings,* she told herself sternly. *But I sure can control my own. No matter what Scott—or anyone else—does to upset me.*

As the two of them came within a few feet of each other, Stevie forced herself to smile. "Hi, Scott," she said politely. "How's it going?"

Scott was clearly taken aback by her greeting. His step faltered, though his expression didn't get any friendlier. Finally, he nodded curtly before hurrying on his way.

Once he was past, Stevie shrugged and sighed. "One day at a time," she muttered as she continued toward the tack room.

Carole was taking her time getting Starlight ready to go. "Did you miss me last week, boy?" she whispered as she carefully untangled a small knot he had managed to get in his silky black mane. "I missed you. I don't care how pretty all those fancy TV horses are, they can't hold a candle to you. I don't know how anyone could think any different."

Starlight just stood calmly, chewing on a mouthful of hay. Carole finished getting rid of the knot, then walked to the front of the stall for the gelding's tack. Outside, she heard someone coming down the aisle in her direction. Thinking it was Stevie returning, she poked her head out.

"That was fast," she called. "You must have run the whole— Oh! Ben. It's you."

"Hi, Carole." Ben paused outside Starlight's stall. "What's up?"

"Not much," she replied automatically. "We're going for a trail ride." She had seen Ben a few times since returning from California, but she hadn't really had a chance to talk to him. *Not that Ben ever does much talking,* she thought.

Still, something was bothering her. It was just a little thing, but it didn't jibe with what Carole knew—or thought she knew—about Ben.

"So," she said, trying to sound casual, "I've been meaning to ask. Did Veronica diAngelo do any more riding while I was away?"

If Ben thought the question was odd, he didn't show it. "Nope." He shrugged. "Haven't seen her since that time before you left."

"Hmmm. Too bad." Carole was watching him closely while pretending to fuss with Starlight's saddle. She knew it was stupid. She knew it was petty. But she couldn't help being disturbed by the positive comments Ben had made about Veronica. After all, Ben didn't seem to like many people—not even nice, friendly people like Scott Forester. Why would he bother to compliment Veronica, of all people?

This time Ben did look slightly surprised by her comment. "That's funny. I thought you didn't like her much."

"I don't," Carole replied shortly. "But you seemed to think she was pretty cool."

Ben shrugged, and for a moment Carole was afraid he wouldn't respond. Then he spoke. "I wouldn't go that far."

"What do you mean?"

Ben shrugged again, seeming reluctant to elaborate. "She's a pretty good rider. Otherwise, she's kind of a jerk."

"You mean you actually noticed?" Carole was stunned. Obviously she had misread Ben once again. "So how come you were so nice to her?"

Ben cast her an inquiring glance. "Why shouldn't I be polite? I don't have to like her to saddle a horse for her. Anyway, she may be a snob, but at least she doesn't try to hide it. She's exactly what she presents herself to be—no games."

It was one of the longer speeches Carole could remember hearing from Ben, and it told her everything she needed to know, including a few things he had left unsaid. Now she understood, and she should have seen it before. If there was one thing Ben couldn't stand, it was hypocrisy. That was why Veronica didn't bother him. For all her faults, it was true that she didn't usually expend much effort trying to convince people she was anything other than what she was. Carole had already guessed that Ben considered Scott Forester a phony, just like his politician father. That kind of thing really rubbed him the wrong way, which was why he'd had it in for Scott from the day they'd met.

Carole didn't agree with Ben about Scott. She wasn't even sure she agreed about Veronica, since she had seen for herself how deceitful and hypocritical Veronica could be when it suited her purposes. But it didn't really matter. She was just relieved that her questions about Ben's taste in people had been cleared up.

Ben moved on, and before long Stevie returned with her new stirrup leather. Soon both horses were ready to go. "We might as well head out, I guess," Stevie said, leading Belle out of her stall.

Carole followed with Belle as Stevie led the way to the lucky horseshoe nailed to the wall near Pine Hollow's main door. The horseshoe had been there for as long as anyone could remember, and it was said that no rider had ever had a serious accident after touching it for luck. The two girls mounted and urged their horses toward the wall until they were close enough to brush the worn metal of the horseshoe with their fingers.

"This is weird, isn't it?" Stevie commented, leaning back in her saddle and gathering up Belle's reins. "I mean, our trail rides haven't seemed the same all summer. And now—"

"Hi, guys!" a breathless voice came from the doorway. "Sorry I'm late."

Carole turned to smile at Lisa. "It's about time," she joked. "We were getting ready to leave without you."

"Sorry," Lisa said again. "You know how my mother is. She claimed we'd just make a quick trip to the mall, but once we got there she decided we had to make up for a whole summer's worth of missed shopping opportunities."

"Don't listen to Carole," Stevie advised. "We already guessed what happened. We were planning to warm up in the outdoor ring until you got here."

Lisa was already heading toward the tack room. "Go ahead," she called over her shoulder. "I'll have Prancer ready in a jiff."

She hurried to follow up on her words, going through the familiar motions of retrieving Prancer's tack, greeting the sweet bay mare, and getting ready to hit the trail.

She was still getting used to being back in Willow Creek, among the sights and sounds she had grown up with, even though she had flown in from L.A. three days earlier. Her decision hadn't been easy, and she had come very close to choosing to stay in California. But in the end, she had opted to return home. She had a full life here with lots of things to look forward to in her senior year. There would be time for new people and places soon enough, when it was time to go to college.

"It wasn't an easy choice, that's for sure," she murmured to Prancer as she tightened her girth. "But I'm glad I forced myself to really think about it. And I think I made the right decision—for now, at least."

She supposed the thought of the opportunities she had passed up would always be a little bittersweet. And she would never know what might have been if she had decided the other way.

Still, she was starting to recognize that the world out there was full of difficult choices. Unless she was willing to accept that, she might as well give up and let other people run her life for her.

She led Prancer out to the stable entrance and mounted. Leaning over to tap the lucky horseshoe, Lisa smiled. The gesture felt so familiar, so automatic—so homey. How many years had it been now that she had been touching that ragged bit of metal, counting on it to bring her good luck?

"But it's not really about luck, is it, girl?" she

murmured to her horse. "It's all about being willing to make a choice."

She patted the mare on the neck and urged her into a trot, eager to join her friends, who were cantering around the ring outside. She couldn't wait to start their trail ride, couldn't wait to get back into the swing of things in her chosen home.

But she paused outside the gate, just long enough to whisper one more thing into the mare's ear. "Here's the greatest part of all, though, Prancer. There's always room to change your mind."

ABOUT THE AUTHOR

BONNIE BRYANT is the author of nearly a hundred books about horses, including The Saddle Club series, Saddle Club Super Editions, and the Pony Tails series. She has also written novels and movie novelizations under her married name, B. B. Hiller.

Ms. Bryant began writing The Saddle Club in 1986. Although she had done some riding before that, she intensified her studies then and found herself learning right along with her characters Stevie, Carole, and Lisa. She claims that they are all much better riders than she is.

Ms. Bryant was born and raised in New York City. She still lives there, in Greenwich Village, with her two sons.

And don't miss the next
PINE HOLLOW book

C H A N G I N G   L E A D S

Stevie Lake can't get Scott Forester to forgive her
for the car accident that injured his sister. And
now Scott and Stevie's boyfriend, Phil, have
started hanging out. Doesn't Phil realize how
Scott's attitude hurts her? But Phil has problems
of his own. His best friend, A.J., is acting weird
and won't tell anyone what's going on. Phil's
getting really worried.

Lisa Atwood is adjusting to life back home
after her summer in California, but she feels like
an outsider—even among her best friends. Will
she have to accept this change?

Carole Hanson is facing changes, too. New
challenges at work mean new responsibilities—
and that threatens her relationship with one of
her best friends. Should Carole reexamine where
her loyalties lie?

Summer may be over, but things are just be-
ginning to heat up.

Coming in January 1999!

Real life. Real friends. Real faith.

Clearwater Crossing—where
friendships are formed, hearts
come together, choices have
consequences, and lives
are changed
forever . . .

#1

#2

#3

#4

~ clearwater crossing ~

An inspirational new series
available now wherever books are sold.

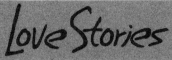